Welcome to Sena Pueblo...

...where the old beliefs still live in high desert country.

...where the Pueblo people believe in the power of a shaman to heal, and in the power of a *brujo* to curse.

...where three former Pueblo bad boys must unite to fight the magic of a murderous witch before he takes the life of another victim.

As teenagers, Luke and Tom and Rico were the terror of the pueblo. But a tragedy forced them to go their separate ways. Now, in an ironic twist of fate, these desert sons must reunite, for only they have the power to save their people and the women they love....

Dear Harlequin Intrigue Reader,

This month you'll want to have all six of our books to keep you company as you brave those April showers!

- Debra Webb kicks off THE ENFORCERS, her exciting new trilogy, with *John Doe on Her Doorstep*. And for all of you who have been waiting with bated breath for the newest installment in Kelsey Roberts's THE LANDRY BROTHERS series, we have *Chasing Secrets*.

- Rebecca York, Ann Voss Peterson and Patricia Rosemoor join together in *Desert Sons*. You won't want to miss this unique three-in-one collection!

- Two of your favorite promotions are back. You won't be able to resist Leona Karr's ECLIPSE title, *Shadows on the Lake*. And you'll be on the edge of your seat while reading Jean Barrett's *Paternity Unknown*, the latest installment in TOP SECRET BABIES.

- Meet another of THE PRECINCT's rugged lawmen in Julie Miller's *Police Business*.

Every month you can depend on Harlequin Intrigue to deliver an array of thrilling romantic suspense and mystery. Be sure you read each one!

Sincerely,

Denise O'Sullivan
Senior Editor
Harlequin Intrigue

REBECCA YORK
ANN VOSS PETERSON
PATRICIA ROSEMOOR

DESERT SONS

RUTH GLICK WRITING AS REBECCA YORK

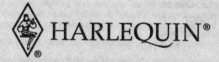

HARLEQUIN®

TORONTO • NEW YORK • LONDON
AMSTERDAM • PARIS • SYDNEY • HAMBURG
STOCKHOLM • ATHENS • TOKYO • MILAN • MADRID
PRAGUE • WARSAW • BUDAPEST • AUCKLAND

ISBN 0-373-22838-4

DESERT SONS

Copyright © 2005 by Harlequin Books S.A.

The publisher acknowledges the copyright holders of the individual works

LUKE
Copyright © 2005 by Ruth Glick

TOM
Copyright © 2005 by Ann Voss Peterson

RICO
Copyright © 2005 by Patricia Pinianski

This edition published by arrangement with Harlequin Books S.A.

® and TM are trademarks of the publisher. Trademarks indicated with ® are registered in the United States Patent and Trademark Office, the Canadian Trade Marks Office and in other countries.

www.eHarlequin.com

Printed in U.S.A.

Rebecca York

Award-winning, bestselling novelist Ruth Glick, who writes as Rebecca York, is the author of close to eighty books, including her popular 43 LIGHT STREET series for Harlequin Intrigue. Ruth says she has the best job in the world. Not only does she get paid for telling stories, she's also the author of twelve cookbooks. Ruth and her husband, Norman, travel frequently, researching locales for her novels and searching out new dishes for her cookbooks.

Ann Voss Peterson

Ever since she was a little girl making her own books out of construction paper, Ann Voss Peterson wanted to write. So when it came time to choose a major at the University of Wisconsin, creative writing was her only choice. Of course, writing wasn't a *practical* choice—one needs to earn a living. So Ann found jobs ranging from proofreading legal transcripts, to working with quarter horses, to washing windows. But no matter how she earned her paycheck, she continued to write the type of stories that captured her heart and imagination—romantic suspense. Ann loves to hear from readers. E-mail her at ann@annvosspeterson.com or visit her Web site at www.annvosspeterson.com.

Patricia Rosemoor

To research her novels, Patricia Rosemoor is willing to swim with dolphins, round up mustangs or howl with wolves... "Whatever it takes to write a credible tale." She's the author of contemporary, historical and paranormal romances, but her first love has always been romantic suspense. Patricia teaches Suspense-Thriller Writing and Writing Popular Fiction at Columbia College Chicago. She lives in Chicago with her husband, Edward, and their three cats. She would love to know what you think of this story. Write her at P.O. Box 578297, Chicago, IL 60657-8297 or via e-mail at Patricia@PatriciaRosemoor.com, and visit her Web site at www.PatriciaRosemoor.com.

CAST OF CHARACTERS

Luke Cordova—After serving time for a crime he didn't commit, the pueblo bad boy thought he'd left his problems behind. But when black magic threatens Ashley Donaldson, he vows to uncover the dark secrets of the past.

Ashley Donaldson—She came back to the pueblo to claim her birthright. Little did she know her heritage was plagued by witchcraft and murder, and that the only man who could save her was the one she never thought she'd love.

Tom Lahi—After his friend was wrongly imprisoned, Tom became a lawyer to fight for justice. But to win this battle, he must believe in an ancient magic…and the power of love.

Jessie Gardner—She rebelled against her wealthy father and joined the FBI. But when she's teamed up with Tom Lahi, who as a boy sent her heart racing, can she stand up to him, too?

Rico Tafoya—The gallery owner turned his back on his heritage after his friend was unjustly incarcerated. But as evil threatens, he can't ignore his love for his people.

Charlotte Reyna—The local artist knows Rico Tafoya is a good man at heart, but can her love convince him to save his people?

Joe Cordova—The famous artist has a dark past—and it has finally caught up with him.

Paxton Gardner—The art collector buys and sells people the way he does Native American art.

Raul Estavez—The potter is desperate to make a name for himself. But how far would he go?

Jay Soto—Rico's overzealous assistant has been caught spying on others at the art gallery. Could he be up to something sinister?

Roberto Sanchez—The janitor will do anything for money.

Fred Gonzales—The tribal police officer takes out his frustrations on everyone around him.

LUKE
REBECCA YORK

RUTH GLICK WRITING AS REBECCA YORK

Prologue

In the darkness, the witch stood outside Joe Cordova's isolated desert house, looking through the lighted windows, watching the artist's shuffling gait as he walked from his studio to the bedroom.

"You've made a mistake, old man. You should have left well enough alone. And don't count on Ashley Donaldson or your nephew, Luke, to save you."

As though he heard the words, the artist went stock-still and stared into the darkness beyond the house. A flash of fear contorted his face. Then he firmed his features and went back to what he had been doing—getting ready for an important art show in Santa Fe.

But he was never going to arrive. He was going to die. By his own hand, if possible. So that the only evidence would be of his own demented state.

In a low voice the witch began to chant—ancient words that had served him well over the years.

Lightning crackled across the velvet sky and wind stirred the piñons. In the desert, a coyote howled.

"Help me, brother. Lend me your cunning," the witch whispered, moving past a tall cactus toward the house.

Inside, the artist stopped again. This time when he raised his head, he couldn't wipe away the fear.

"Go away," he called into the darkness. "Leave me alone."

The witch answered with a burst of mental energy—of defiance. Of anger. Of power.

And the man staggered back, throwing his hands in front of his face. As though flesh and blood could protect him.

The witch spewed forth another burst of anger and the traitor screamed in pain and terror.

Chapter One

Ashley Donaldson hurried from the parking lot behind Canyon Road and up the steps to the Milagro Gallery. She'd been tied up with a client and now she was late to the opening.

Pushing open one of the heavy carved doors, she stepped onto the pegged wood floor—then went very still as she was enveloped by the sounds, the scents, the sights of New Mexico. The mix of acoustic guitar and Native American flutes. The aroma of piñon from a burning smudge stick.

Through the well-dressed crowd, she caught glimpses of the paintings and sculpture filling the rooms. Adorning the walls were desert landscapes and craggy mountains kissed by the last rays of the setting sun. On pedestals and in glass cases in the center of the room were three-dimensional pieces: a beautifully executed black-and-white pot, a tawny mountain lion about to spring, turquoise-and-silver jewelry.

That she was here, in this environment, never failed to amaze her. She'd grown up in L.A.—the adopted daughter of Marge and Cal Donaldson. But after college she'd longed to learn about her heritage. So she'd come back to Sena Pueblo, her birth mother's home, and she'd been here for the past two years.

"Ashley."

She glanced around and spotted gallery owner Rico Tafoya striding toward her. His long black hair was pulled back in a braid lashed with a leather thong and decorated with a single raven's feather. His shirt, pants and boots were black, too, set off by silver-and-turquoise jewelry. He looked the very image of a successful mestizo entrepreneur selling Native American works in Santa Fe.

"I'm glad you could come," he said, clasping her hand.

Rico had grown up in the pueblo. His mixed heritage had given him striking features, while her own brown hair and brown eyes were nothing special.

Rico's face turned angry as he peered around her. "So where's Joe?" he asked gruffly.

She blinked. "Isn't he here already?"

"No. I thought you might be bringing him. What's he trying to pull?"

Ashley fought confusion.

"Forget it," Rico said in the next breath.

"Maybe he's with Luke," she suggested.

"Maybe."

So what was going on between Rico and Joe? Joe was an artist and one of her anchors to New Mexico. He'd been in love with her mother twenty-seven years ago and had offered to marry her when she'd gotten pregnant by a cowboy drifter. But she'd taken off for L.A. instead, and Joe hadn't even known what had happened to her and the baby—until Ashley had come back to the pueblo.

In the two years that she'd been in New Mexico, she and Joe had become close friends. For the past few weeks she'd known he was upset about something—although he hadn't shared his concerns with her. Was he feuding with Rico?

This wasn't the time to ask, especially when wealthy art patrons Paxton and Kathleen Gardner were coming toward them. A few paces behind was a slender blond with short-cropped hair, wearing a severe pantsuit instead of a party dress. It was their daughter, Jessie. She had grown up in the area and had become an FBI agent, much against her parents' wishes. She was probably trying to make some brownie points with them by attending the show.

"Wonderful opening," Paxton said in a hearty voice. "Charlotte Reyna has outdone herself. I'm thinking about buying one of her landscapes."

Ashley wandered away, nibbling on a mini blue-corn tortilla as she admired the paintings and sculptures. But she kept one eye on the door, looking for Joe—or even Luke, though, to tell the truth, Joe's nephew wasn't her favorite person. Luke walked around with a ten-pound chip on his shoulder, although she certainly understood why.

Charlotte Reyna caught her eye and Ashley crossed the room. "I hear Paxton Gardner is interested in your work," Ashley murmured.

Charlotte flipped a lock of long, dark hair behind her ear. "Yes! He's put a reserve on one of my three canvases."

"Way to go!"

Charlotte accepted the congratulations graciously. She and Ashley were friends. About the same age, they'd both returned to Sena Pueblo as adults. And they were both still trying to find their way in a world where neither was entirely comfortable.

Roberto Sanchez nodded to Ashley as he took a plastic bag of used cups and paper plates from a trash receptacle and replaced it with a fresh bag.

"How is your sister?" Ashley asked.

"Doing better, thanks to you," Roberto said. His sister, Anita Morales, had been rushed to a local hospital recently for stomach pains and had needed an emergency appendectomy. As part of her job at Pueblo Aid, Ashley had straightened out the insurance payment.

She kept moving through the gallery, looking for Joe, her uneasiness about his absence mounting. Someone waved at her across the room and she waved back. It was potter Raul Estevez, whom she hadn't seen until now.

Raul was a buddy of Joe's and she wondered if he might know where Joe was. But before she could cross to him, the crowd swallowed him up again, and she knew she wasn't going to be able to relax until she drove out to the pueblo to see if her friend was okay.

Turning back to Charlotte, she said, "If Joe comes in, could you give me a call on my cell phone?"

"Sure. Where are you going?"

"To check on one of my clients," she said, not wanting to worry Charlotte on this important night in her career.

"What about Luke?" Charlotte asked with a little smile.

"What about him?"

"He'll be looking for you."

"I doubt it." She and Joe's nephew tolerated each other—barely.

Luke had been a juvenile delinquent in his youth and had finally gotten arrested at nineteen by the tribal police for a robbery he hadn't committed. Unfortunately he'd spent five years in jail until the real perpetrator had confessed.

The experience could have destroyed him, but when he'd gotten out of jail, Joe had helped to set him up as a handyman. As his projects had become bigger, he'd transformed himself into a contractor—with a reputation for personalized service.

She knew Joe wanted her and Luke to be friends. But the guy always seemed so cold and distant—with a way of mocking her that set her nerves on edge—so she'd given up on any kind of relationship.

It was after nine when Ashley stepped outside into the cold, clear evening and dragged in a breath of mountain air.

Thousands of stars twinkled above her. She took a moment to admire them, then descended the steps to the parking lot, thinking how far she was from the smoggy skies of her childhood.

Away from the music and conversation, she used her cell phone to call Joe—and got his answering machine.

"In case you're on your way to the opening, I'll see you there," she said, thinking that if she didn't find him at home, her only alternative was to make the trek back to Santa Fe.

Canyon Road, Santa Fe's Gallery Row, was a one-way street, and she had a little trouble getting to the highway because she didn't know this area of town very well. Unable to tamp down her tension, she sped toward Sena Pueblo, hoping she wouldn't get pulled over by a cop.

At the two-lane road that led to the small community, she slowed her speed. She'd visited other pueblos since coming to New Mexico. A few, like Taos, reminded her of ancient apartment buildings, the adobe-brick housing units stacked together like giant blocks. But in Sena, most of the houses were low, separate structures grouped around an unpaved recreation area. The police station and the other public buildings, such as the Pueblo Affairs office, were in a small complex slightly removed from the residential area.

With the money rolling in from his paintings, Joe had built himself a very upscale home, in traditional southwest style, occupying a patch of desert about ten minutes from the heart of the community.

She saw the low adobe house miles before she arrived. Every light was shining into the darkness as if he owned stock in the electric company. But as she neared the dwelling, she couldn't see anyone inside.

Lord, had he suffered a heart attack? Had he fallen? Or was he in some other kind of trouble?

After pulling to a stop next to the artist's shiny new SUV, she leaped from the car and ran toward the carved wooden door. When no one answered her knock, she reached for the brass knob.

The door was unlocked so she yanked it open and stepped onto the thick Mexican tile of the foyer.

"Joe?"

He didn't answer.

"Joe?"

A blur of movement made her head jerk up—as the man himself leaped out of the shadows in the hallway, his eyes wild, a revolver in his hand.

Chapter Two

She froze.

"Joe, it's all right. It's Ashley," she soothed, hearing the quaver in her own voice as she studied the terrible tension in his weathered face. "It's Ashley," she repeated, because he didn't seem to recognize her. "I'm here to help you."

"No! Get away from me."

Joe Cordova was as familiar to her as her own adopted parents. But tonight his eyes were wide and staring.

"Stay away," he warned, lifting the gun.

She didn't know what to do. Back up? Or hold her ground? So she stood where she was, her heart blocking her windpipe, wondering if this man who had been like a favorite uncle to her was going to kill her.

"Please, take it easy," she whispered, her voice high and thin. "Can you tell me what's wrong?"

He didn't seem to be listening. When she reached a hand toward him, he raised the gun. "Stay back!" he warned.

Her only defense was to stand stock-still—fighting the impulse to throw her hands protectively in front of her body.

Her friend might have shot her. Instead some small measure of sanity flickered in his eyes.

"No," he said again, this time sounding as though his meaning might have changed. She was about to plead with him to put the gun down when he turned and whirled away.

As he rushed down the hall, Ashley let out the breath she hadn't known she was holding. She knew the house. The hall led to the kitchen and family room combination, then to the bedrooms and the art studio. She had to go after him, find out what was wrong.

Hearing a squeaking sound, she pictured the sliding-glass door in the family room moving in its track. The door led to the patio. Was he going out—into the desert night?

She was on her way down the hall when footsteps sounded behind her, and she started to turn.

When hard fingers clamped around her arm, holding her in place, she gasped.

She tried to wrench away, but the hand held her fast, turned her—and she found herself staring into the dark, questioning eyes of Luke Cordova.

He seemed to tower over her, dark and lean and angry. "What the hell is going on here, *chiquita?*" he asked. "Why are all the lights on? What are you doing here?"

As usual, Luke Cordova had arrived with an attitude.

LUKE WATCHED Ashley steady herself, dragging in a breath and letting it out before answering his urgent questions. "Honestly, I'm not sure what's going on. We need to check the back door."

He was still holding her arm. Deliberately he loosened his grasp and let her lead him along the hall.

When they reached the family room, he saw that the sliding-glass door was wide open.

She pointed. "I think Joe ran out there."

"And you let him go out into the desert—at night?" he asked, hearing the accusing tone of his own voice.

She raised her chin. "I didn't have much choice. He had a gun. He pointed it at me and warned me to stay where I was."

A strangled exclamation rose in his throat. "He threatened *you?*"

"Yes."

Abandoning her, Luke charged onto the wide patio, filled with heavy wooden furniture and huge ceramic pots of bougainvillea and other flowering plants. When she followed, he half turned and growled, "Get back inside!"

To his annoyance, she stayed where she was. When he turned again, he felt as if she were staring at the back of his neck where his dark hair was pulled back into a short ponytail.

He'd been startled to find her here. He didn't know how to deal with her presence—or with what she'd said had happened.

Trying to ignore her, he cupped his hands around his mouth. "Joe? Are you out here, Joe?"

Only the mournful sound of the wind answered.

He stepped into the darkness.

"Be careful," Ashley called, her voice high and strained—like she cared about what happened to him.

"Yeah."

In the light shining from the window, he searched the exterior of the house, trying to calm the pounding of his heart.

He'd had a bad feeling tonight—even before he'd talked to Rico. It wasn't getting any better. Joe was out here with a gun. And if Ashley was right, his uncle had lost his marbles.

He gave up after twenty minutes, knowing that if

Joe wanted to avoid being found, he could damn well do it. He knew the desert as well as he knew the inside of his own house.

When he returned to the family room and closed the door, he found Ashley huddled on the worn leather sofa that Joe had owned since Luke was a boy. He could feel Joe's presence in the room. In the artwork—his own and other artists'—hanging on the rough walls. In the priceless woven rugs on the wooden floor. In the kiva-style fireplace dominating a corner of the room.

But Ashley dominated the room just by her presence. She looked fragile in the pretty white dress she must have worn to the art gallery. That was an illusion, he told himself. Really, she was tough and determined, or she wouldn't be working at the pueblo helping residents with everything from food stamp applications to legal problems.

"What are you doing at Joe's house, *chiquita?*" he asked, hating the gruffness of his voice.

"Don't call me '*chiquita,*'" she snapped. "At least, not in that tone of voice."

She had never protested the teasing name before. Having made her point, she went on. "I was at the art show opening, waiting for Joe. When he didn't arrive, I got worried, so I came to look for him. I found him in the house…" She stopped and swallowed. "He looked…terrified. He had a gun. He pointed it at me. I got the feeling he didn't even know who I was. Then he turned and ran down the hall. I heard the sliding-glass door open. The next thing I knew, you had a hand clamped around my arm."

He nodded, standing with his shoulder propped against the wall, keeping his distance from her.

ASHLEY CLAMBERED OFF the sofa, trying to put herself on an equal footing with Luke, even as she silently admitted that nothing would ever make her feel equal to Luke Cordova. He wasn't tall. Only a few inches taller than her own five-six height. But his shoulders were broad. His body was lean and muscular. And his deep-set dark eyes always gave her the impression that he was seeing more than she wanted.

She'd never figured out if he thought she was inter-fering in Joe's life, if he was jealous of her relationship or if he was treating her with his normal hostility.

He was wearing his usual outfit—a dark T-shirt, jeans and boots, and she wondered if he'd been plan-ning to attend the opening looking as though he was dressed for work.

"How did you end up out here?" she asked.

"I called Rico, and he told me Joe hadn't arrived. As soon as I finished with tonight's plumbing emergency, I came over."

She nodded, knowing that he often put his clients' needs before his own. That was one of the reasons he'd become so successful. He also had a reputation for hir-ing men from the pueblo who might not be able to get jobs with anyone else. Men who came from back-grounds similar to his own.

"You can go back to the festivities," he said.

She blinked, wondering if she'd heard him correctly. "Don't you think I'm worried about Joe?"

"Maybe. But you don't have to hang around. I can handle things out here."

She lifted one shoulder. "The show is probably over by now. And I have no intention of leaving—until I find out what's wrong with Joe."

He shrugged. "Suit yourself."

When he started turning off lights, she did the same, darkening most of the rooms in the front of the house, while he took the back. They met in the family room again. Ignoring her, he strode to the coffee machine in the kitchen and poured himself a mug.

"You drink coffee this late at night?" she asked.

"When I plan to stay up." He took a sip of the brew.

Until that moment she hadn't thought about the implication, that the two of them would be spending the night alone in a deserted house—unless the owner reappeared. And maybe he'd come charging through the door with his gun drawn. Which meant that going to sleep wouldn't be such a great idea.

She joined Luke in the kitchen, poured herself half a mug of Joe's strong coffee, then added almost as much milk and a spoonful of sugar before carrying the mug back to the sofa and taking a cautious sip.

Luke took the matching leather easy chair, fixing her again with that unnerving stare of his.

Trying not to shift in her seat, she asked, "How has Joe seemed to you lately?"

"Preoccupied. How has he seemed to you?"

"Worried. Does he confide in you?"

"Not about his problems," Luke allowed.

She nodded, thinking that Joe had been such a good friend to her, but he hadn't asked for anything in return. He'd just seemed glad that she'd come back to the home she'd never really known.

Luke cleared his throat. "Go on and get some sleep. I'll stay up."

"I will, too," she murmured. Not because she wanted to keep him company.

Feeling overdressed in the white Mexican-style party frock she'd worn to the gallery, she thought about changing into something more comfortable. Luckily, she had some clothing in the spare bedroom, since she sometimes spent the weekend out here.

Excusing herself, she went to change into jeans, a long-sleeved shirt and running shoes.

She was just buttoning the shirt when the sound of an animal howling in the darkness made the hair on the back of her neck bristle.

Hurrying back to the family room, she found that Luke had turned off the remaining lights and was standing at the window, staring out.

THE SOUND OF FOOTSTEPS behind him made Luke whirl.

"What was that?" Ashley asked.

"A coyote," he answered, even when he didn't know if he was speaking the truth.

Before he could say more, the frantic beating of wings outside the window sent goose bumps dancing over his skin. It sounded like a large bird of prey circling the house, getting ready to attack.

Then, from one eye blink to the next, the bird was no longer on the other side of the glass. It was right in the room, flapping and swooping and calling out in anger.

He wanted to believe it had somehow flown down the chimney. But he couldn't make himself buy it.

All he could think was that he must protect Ashley. Leaping toward her, he pulled her into his arms, bending over her body as he sought to merge her form against his own.

In the darkened room he could see nothing. But he could hear the beating of wings, feel currents of air move as an unearthly screech filled the space around him.

He had never felt comfortable with Ashley Donaldson. She was so far beyond his experience that he'd never known what to say to her—how to treat her. Tonight he gathered her close, comforting and shielding her.

As quickly as the assault had started, it stopped.

For long moments neither of them spoke or moved. He could hear her gasping for breath.

Finally she brought her hands up and pressed against his shoulders. When he realized he was still clasping her as though they had suddenly become lovers, he dropped his arms to his sides and stepped back.

"What was that?" she whispered.

This time when he answered he tried to be as honest as he could. "A ghost. Or a witch."

"You're serious?" she breathed.

"What else could it be?"

She stared up at him. "You believe in…in witches?"

"My people believe in witches…transforming themselves into animals to do evil. An owl. A coyote."

"My people, too," she murmured. "It isn't my fault that I wasn't raised here."

"But it's hard to believe in…superstitions…if you haven't lived here on the pueblo all your life."

Ignoring the observation she said, "A bird came down the chimney."

"Yeah, it would be convenient to think that, too. But where did it go?"

She couldn't answer.

"You should leave," he heard himself say again.

"No."

"Someone is after Joe. If you stay at his house, you could get hurt."

"You, too," she noted.

"I'm willing to take my chances," he said evenly.

She gave him a defiant look. "So am I."

He made a rough sound. "You don't know what you're getting into."

"Unlike you?" she challenged.

"I don't know, either!"

"But you're big and strong and can cope with witchcraft!"

He glared at her. "I'm trying to protect you."

"I appreciate that," she answered, sounding like she was lying.

After several charged seconds she returned to the sofa. He went back to the chair, frowning hard.

Maybe because he wanted her to leave, he said, "Did you ever hear the story of how the witch caught his enemy on his way home from a hunting trip in the desert?"

"No. But I'm sure you're going to tell me."

"He took the shape of a coyote and nipped at his heels. The man dropped the meat he was carrying. But that wasn't enough for the witch. He drove the man farther and farther into the desert. And they found his body days later."

"So that's a witch story they tell little kids around here?"

"Yeah."

"And you're telling it to me to get me to go home?"

"Yeah," he admitted again.

"How do they know it was a witch—if it happened out in the desert?"

"From the look of terror in the man's dead eyes."

She made a snorting sound. "That's a great story. But I'm not leaving unless you are."

"Then I guess we're stuck with each other."

"Why would a witch come after Joe?" she finally asked.

"I don't know!" He wanted to pace back and forth across the room. But there were no drapes on the sliding-glass doors facing the desert. If he moved around in here, even with the lights off, he would make them both a target for anyone outside with a gun or a witch's spell.

So they sat facing each other in tense silence.

As the night dragged on, he watched Ashley slip lower in her seat. Watched her get more comfortable. And finally he watched her sleep, listening to the even sound of her breathing. He wanted to cross the room and move so that his shoulder was pressed to hers. He wanted do more, if he were honest, but he sat in the leather chair, his hands clutching the arms.

He was angry with himself. He was worried about Joe. The only person who had believed in him—when he hadn't even believed in himself. But he couldn't keep his mind off the woman sleeping across the room from him. A woman who couldn't possibly be interested in a guy like Luke Cordova.

To distract himself, he tiptoed down the hall to the studio. Joe's oil paintings were hung and stacked against the walls. Switching on a light, he looked at each of them—shuffling their positions, thinking they were as familiar as his uncle's face.

Many were of two recurring desert scenes. One was a narrow canyon below soaring towers of brown basalt.

The other showed a major rockfall, a jumble of house-size boulders that had crashed down from the cliffs above. And beyond, an old lava flow, streaking the cliff orange. A stream trickled through the rocks. Sometimes it was in the background, sometimes it was the focus of the painting.

He spent a long time admiring Joe's artistry. When he looked up, the gray light of dawn glimmered through the window.

Finally he abandoned the studio and walked up the

hall to the front of the house, thinking that he might as well get a change of clothing out of his SUV.

The mundane thought fled his mind as he stared at the parking area. Then he let loose with an angry curse.

Chapter Three

Behind him, Luke heard Ashley scurry down the hall.

"What? Did you find Joe?" she asked, her voice soft with sleep.

"Not hardly." He grimaced. "The situation just got worse. He must have rolled his SUV down the hill so we wouldn't hear him, then started the engine. He's gone."

"Gone where?"

He considered the question before saying, "I might have an idea."

As soon as the words were out of his mouth, he wished he'd kept silent.

"Where?" she demanded.

He sighed. "Have you ever taken a good look at his paintings?"

"Of course!"

Luke walked back down the hall. Ashley followed. In the studio, he pointed to the canvases and asked, "What do you see?"

She studied the works. "Magnificent landscapes that make the desert come alive."

"Do you recognize the location?" he prompted.

She gestured toward the two groupings he'd made. "No. But I see two different places."

"Right. They're both in Black Canyon."

"You're thinking he could be there?"

"Since I don't have any better ideas, it's a starting place."

Before he could say more, the sound of an engine had them both running eagerly back to the parking area. But the pickup that had pulled to a stop didn't belong to Joe.

Containing his disappointment, Luke waited tensely as Raul Estevez climbed out and came toward them.

"Is everything okay out here?"

Luke wedged his hands on his hips. "Why do you ask?"

"Because the old buzzard didn't show up last night and word got around that you were worried about him," he said, addressing himself to Ashley. "It's not like him to skip a gallery show. Is he sick or something?"

"He's missing," Luke clipped out.

"And we're still worried about him," Ashley added.

Luke noted that she had sense enough not to mention the gun.

The potter gave them a sympathetic look. "Yeah, Joe has been acting kind of addled lately."

"What have you noticed?" Ashley asked.

"Nothing I could testify to in a court of law," the other man allowed. "But something is eating at him."

"You've been friends for a long time. You have any idea what might be troubling him?" Luke pressed.

Raul shrugged, but Luke got the feeling that Estevez was holding something back, something he might not want to share in front of Ashley.

"We were going out to look for him."

"Do you want me to help?" Estevez asked.

"We'd appreciate it," Ashley answered. "Luke says—"

When Luke grabbed her arm, she stopped speaking—and shot him a questioning look.

"Okay, why don't I go down toward Albuquerque," the potter said. "He heads out that way sometimes."

"Good idea."

Raul climbed back into his truck. Ashley waited until he was driving away from the house before asking, "Why did you stop me from telling him where we might go?"

"Because I've learned that the less you tell people about your business, the better," he replied.

"Why?"

He didn't answer. "Look, we should take the road toward Black Canyon—at least as far as we can get by car. I hope Joe wasn't rash enough to take off across country without water."

When she nodded, he added, "And we should grab something to eat and drink, because rushing off into the desert unprepared is never a smart idea." As he said it, he hoped she'd change her mind about going at all. But she didn't volunteer to back out.

FORTY MINUTES LATER, Ashley sat in the passenger seat beside Luke Cordova as they sped down a narrow road into the desert. He'd made her choke down some eggs and melon for breakfast. Then he'd packed some bottles of water for their trip while she'd called her office at Pueblo Aid and told them that she had a personal emergency.

She cast him a sidewise glance as he drove into the glare of the sun. He reminded her of men she'd encountered on her job. Men who felt there was no way to make a mark in life except by making trouble. But with Joe's help, Luke had escaped the fate of many of her clients.

He was silent as they passed an abandoned adobe church. She wanted to ask him what he was thinking. In a way, they'd gotten closer than she would have believed possible last night. Now he was shutting her out again.

When they rounded a curve between towering brown rocks, something made a sharp, cracking sound in the air above the SUV.

Luke skidded to a stop, pulling off the road and into the protection of the rocks. The sound came again and this time she realized that someone was shooting at them.

"Keep down," Luke shouted. "Get out of the car."

Without questioning his judgment, she pushed her door open, then rolled into a ditch, glad nobody had broken a bottle along the side of the road.

Luke was right behind her, leaping across to the passenger side of the vehicle, then out the door, bracing his weight on his hands as he lowered himself on top of her, covering her body with his.

"Someone's using us for target practice," she heard herself say, knowing she was stating the obvious.

"Yeah. Now keep down."

He spoke with his mouth inches from her ear. If she had turned her head, her lips would have collided with his. So she remained where she was, reassured by the weight of his body on top of hers. Yet she knew that he was putting himself in danger by protecting her. "What are we going to do?" she whispered.

"You're going to stay out of the line of fire. I'll try to get behind him."

"Is it Joe?" She asked the terrible question hovering in her mind.

"I don't know," he answered, sounding as anguished as she felt.

"Stay down. Keep the SUV between you and them," Luke warned, then lifted up enough to reach into the glove compartment.

When he came back down to the ground, she saw that he was holding an automatic.

She eyed the gun, not really surprised. In this country, most men were armed.

Luke disappeared from sight behind a rock and her heart leaped into her throat.

He had told her to stay down. But she couldn't just let him put himself in danger. Rising up a little, she reached into the SUV and pulled out her purse, then fumbled inside for her cell phone.

She jumped back into the ditch, sweat dripping down her face and neck, mixing with the dust. She tried to call 9-1-1 and got static. Apparently the bottom of a rocky canyon wasn't the best place for reception.

The sound of another gunshot made her blood freeze.

She couldn't see what was happening. She couldn't even see who was shooting. All she could think was that Luke might be in danger.

Chapter Four

Ashley ached to call out to Luke. She ached to know that he was all right. But raising her voice would put them both in danger.

Finally, when she couldn't bear the suspense, she wormed her way toward the rocks, then waited for several seconds before cautiously standing.

Far above her a jet plane streaked across the sky, reminding her that civilization hovered not far from this uninhabited patch of New Mexico desert.

She moved cautiously from rock to rock, then peered toward an open area.

In the glaring sunlight she tried to figure out what she was seeing.

A man stood on the edge of a cliff.

Another man lay on the ground at his feet.

"Luke!"

He whirled toward her and, for the second time in eighteen hours, she found herself staring down the barrel of a gun.

"What are you doing here?"

His voice grated as he lowered the gun.

"I…"

The look of sadness on his face had her scrambling

forward. Joe lay on the ground, a bullet hole in the side of his head.

She gasped and would have gone to her knees, but Luke kept her standing.

"Don't!"

"I have to…"

"He's dead. You can't do anything for him."

Tears filmed her eyes as she looked down at the man who had made such a difference in her life. It was hard to believe he was dead. But the evidence was right in front of her.

"Was he shooting at us? Did he kill himself?" she managed to ask.

"I don't know," he answered, gesturing toward Joe's hand, which hung off the edge of the cliff. "If he was holding his gun, it's at the bottom of the cliff."

Ashley nodded numbly. "We have to…"

"Call the authorities," Luke finished.

"I tried to use my cell phone. It wouldn't work."

Luke reached into his pants pocket and pulled out his phone. When he flipped it open and pressed the on button, he cursed.

"What?"

"I was going to recharge it last night. But I forgot about that—at Joe's." The look on his face was stark as he said, "We have to go to the tribal police."

"Yes," she answered automatically. In truth, she didn't know what to do. "Should we…should we take Joe with us?" she murmured.

"No. Don't you watch television? We shouldn't disturb the…crime scene any more than we have to."

She took a step back, wavering on her feet, and Luke moved quickly forward, steadying her with an arm around her waist. "Are you okay?"

"No. Are you?"

"No."

The conversation ground to a halt as he helped her back to the SUV.

"He was a good man," she murmured as the two of them headed back toward the pueblo.

Luke nodded, his face reflecting both sadness and anger.

She wanted to keep the conversation going, but his body language made it clear he wasn't interested. Just before they reached the tribal police station, he spoke.

"When we talk to the cops, I don't want to talk about what happened last night. I mean, about…the witch."

"Why not?"

"Joe is dead. If we start babbling about witches, they're going to wonder if we're on drugs or something."

Last night he'd said his people believed in the supernatural. This morning he was saying that didn't include tribal policemen. But she realized this wasn't the time to question his logic.

"Okay," she murmured. "But what do I say about Joe's threatening me?"

"You have to make that decision."

She nodded, wondering what she was going to say. Then she looked up as they pulled into the parking area in front of the small adobe building.

When she saw who was standing outside, she made a disgusted sound. Tribal policeman Fred Gonzales was leaning against one of the porch posts, smoking what looked like a hand-rolled cigarette.

In her job she'd worked with a number of tribal cops. Most were good men. But the short, beefy Gonzales gave her nightmares. He liked to throw his weight around, liked to make sure you knew who was top dog.

He looked up with interest as Luke cut the engine.

"I should have left you out of this," he muttered.

"You can't. I'm a witness."

"Yeah," he conceded as they exited the vehicle.

Gonzales took one last drag on his cigarette, flipped it to the ground and crushed it under his boot as he looked inquiringly at Luke.

"To what do I owe this pleasure? You turning yourself in for some crime?" he asked, then laughed at his own hilarious joke.

Ashley glanced at the set lines of Luke's face. When she saw his hand clench, she reached down and captured it in her own, holding tight.

Gonzales looked with interest at the gesture. "You two an item?"

"We're here to report a death," Ashley snapped.

The cop straightened. "Let's have it."

Luke answered. "We just found Joe Cordova—dead—out near the road to Black Canyon."

"What were you doing out there?" Gonzales demanded. "Drugs?"

Luke's jaw hardened and Ashley couldn't believe that Gonzales would have said something so confrontational—or that he'd zeroed in on drugs the way Luke had suggested he would.

He managed to keep his voice even. "After Joe didn't show up at the art gallery last night, we were worried about him. We both went out to his house, looking for him."

"Was he home?"

Ashley swallowed, not sure what to say. Finally she decided on some version of the truth. "He was there. But he was upset. He wouldn't tell me what was bothering him. Before Luke arrived, he ran outside."

"In the morning, we started searching for him," Luke added quickly.

Gonzales smirked. "You spent the night at his house—together?"

"Yes, but not how you think," Ashley snapped. This man was making it difficult to hang on to her temper. Deliberately she changed the subject. "Somebody shot at us out on the road."

"Oh, yeah?"

"Yes! We pulled over, and Luke went to investigate. That's when we found Joe's body. I assume you want to see where he died."

"I don't need you to tell me how to do my job," Gonzales barked. He turned to Luke. "You show me where you found him."

"Right."

Ashley tightened her hold on his hand, torn. She should let Luke and Gonzales do this, yet she wanted to be there, too. In the end she decided it would be better to keep her nose out of the investigation as much as possible. "Come back and get me when you're finished," she said quietly to Luke. "I'll be at work—unless it's late."

"Okay." He gave her hand a squeeze, then pulled away. "Let's go," he said to Gonzales.

ASHLEY CALLED one of her co-workers for a ride back to Joe's to pick up her car. Then she spent the remainder of the morning and the afternoon alternately crying over Joe and picturing Luke in the desert with Gonzales. Five minutes with the officer had put her on edge. When she pictured the creep trying to goad Luke into doing something foolish, she felt her jaw tighten.

Deliberately she relaxed her muscles. She had never considered Luke Cordova an ally, but they both loved Joe.

When he finally walked into her office just before five o'clock, he looked terrible. Hot and tired and beaten down, with stray strands of hair escaping the band at the back of his neck. She jumped up, facing him across the desk.

"You look awful," she whispered.

"Thanks."

"You need to take a shower and relax."

"I guess I smell like I've spent the day in a sweat lodge."

"No," she said quickly. "But a shower will make you feel better."

"Yeah."

She cleared her throat. "Where...where did they take Joe?"

"The medical investigator facility at the University of New Mexico School of Medicine—in Albuquerque. I couldn't get them to tell me when they'd...release the body," he said, the emotion in his voice tearing at her.

To say "I'm sorry" sounded inadequate, but she said it anyway.

"Not your fault."

"What about the gun? Did you tell them about it?"

"Yeah. The cops were going to climb down into the canyon to look for it. Then Gonzales said that the cliff wall was unstable. So they put it off." He grimaced. "I'm not sure Gonzales believes anybody else was out there."

Chapter Five

Ashley heard herself say, "We should talk over dinner."

Luke hesitated and finally said, "I'll pick you up."

Which was how she found herself twenty minutes later standing in front of her bedroom closet, trying to decide what to wear. Nothing too fancy. This wasn't a date or anything. Finally she settled on a simple black dress with a patterned shawl. Because she was ready early, she had plenty of time to feel her chest tighten with an attack of the jitters.

When she opened the door to Luke's knock at seven, she found him standing on her small front landing, looking as nervous as she felt. She'd never seen him in anything but a T-shirt and jeans, but he was wearing black slacks and a blue button-down shirt that accented his dark good looks. His ponytail was neatly back in place.

Her hand fluttered. "Come in."

He stood where he was for another few seconds, looking at her, and she wondered if he'd changed his mind. Finally he stepped across the threshold, glancing around her small living-dining room area, inspecting her garage sale and thrift shop purchases. She'd found good secondhand furniture, then splurged on some pottery, baskets and watercolors from local artists she admired.

The place of honor over the couch was occupied by one of Joe's paintings that he'd insisted on giving her. It showed the patio of his own home, bright with pots of flowers.

Luke walked toward it. "He gave me a similar painting."

"Something personal." She cleared her throat, feeling herself getting weepy. If she started crying over Joe again, she might not stop. "It's going to be hard getting along without him," she said sadly.

Luke stuck his hands into his pockets. "You could go back to L.A."

The observation shocked her. "I've grown to love New Mexico."

"That must upset your parents."

"If they'd wanted to hide my background, they could have made it hard for me to find out where I came from. But they were always supportive of my…curiosity. They know I don't love them less because I needed to come here…" She stopped, shrugged, wondering why she was trying to tell Luke Cordova how it felt to be torn between two different worlds and to fit into neither. "We should go," she said.

He nodded and turned toward the door. He was driving the same SUV from this morning. And she couldn't help thinking about their narrow escape—and of the way he'd protected her by covering her body with his.

Probably nothing personal, she told herself, judging from the way he was acting now.

She hadn't asked where they were going. He headed back toward Sena Pueblo—to a modern shopping complex not far from the casino. Back to his home territory.

From the outside, the restaurant looked pretty ordinary. But she'd been here to lunch for an office birthday party and knew that behind the plain glass door, it took on a warm southwest atmosphere, with Mexican tiles on the floor, chili peppers hanging from the rafters, and heavy wooden tables and chairs.

The owner nodded to her, then greeted Luke with a bear hug. "I was so sorry to hear about Joe," he said as he led them to a quiet corner.

"You and he are friends?" Ashley asked after they'd been seated.

"Last year, he needed some cash, so I bought into the restaurant. I'm a silent partner," Luke said.

"Oh." She knew Luke had helped out many people on the pueblo. She hadn't known it had included keeping this restaurant afloat.

As though he were following her thoughts, he said, "It was a good investment. And I like having somewhere near home where I can get a quiet meal."

"As opposed to the casino across the way," she guessed.

"Yeah. That's a little loud for my tastes. And I'd feel better about it if my people didn't gamble there."

She nodded, thinking there was a lot she didn't know about Luke Cordova.

The waitress took their drink orders; both she and Luke asked for iced tea. When the drinks arrived, they ordered the Sena combination plate—a selection of the Indian and New Mexican dishes that she'd gotten to like.

"How well do you know Charlotte Reyna?" Luke asked as he dipped a *sopaipilla,* a piece of fried dough, into honey.

"She and I are friends."

"She and Joe were rivals for display space at several galleries, *chiquita.*"

She reared back in her chair. "What are you implying?"

He shrugged, but the look in his eyes told her he was thinking about Charlotte as a suspect.

"Well, how well do you know Rico Tafoya?" she demanded. If he could casually make comments about Charlotte, she could come up with her own theories.

"He and I—and another friend—were the terrors of the pueblo when we were teenagers. Why do you ask?"

"When I came in last night, he seemed angry with Joe."

"He has nothing to do with his murder!"

"You're sure it was murder?"

"I can't prove it. But I think so."

She might have said they both wanted to believe that Joe wouldn't shoot at them—then take his own life. But she closed her mouth abruptly as Fred Gonzales came striding toward them.

"The cozy couple," he said, grinning like a big ape. He was out of uniform, wearing jeans and a T-shirt. Ashley couldn't help but wonder if perhaps he hadn't had a few too many drinks.

She longed to tell him to shove off, instead she replied quietly, "We're having dinner."

"Discussing that famous gun that Luke said Joe had?"

"He did! At least, somebody shot at us," she answered.

"So you say."

Across from her, Luke looked as though he wanted to leap out of his seat and punch the grinning baboon.

To warn him to calm down, she slid her foot under the table and brushed her shoe against his boot. His gaze shot to her.

"Strange that you were around when Joe got into trouble," Gonzales observed.

"Are you implying something?" another voice asked. Ashley glanced up and saw Tom Lahi, his dark hair worn short, the sleeves of his white button-down shirt rolled up. He was standing behind the lawman, his booted foot thrust forward. He was one of the few pueblo men who had gone to law school and returned home to practice. She knew him because he'd defended a lot of her clients pro bono. He nodded politely to her.

"No, I'm not implying anything." Gonzales sneered as he answered the question.

She watched Tom and Luke exchange glances.

"Then I suggest you allow Mr. Cordova and Miss Donaldson to enjoy their dinner."

"Mr. Cordova," Gonzales snarled under his breath as he wove his way toward the door.

Luke stood. He and Tom clasped hands. It was a simple gesture, but a clear indication of a deep friendship.

"How are you doing?" Tom asked.

"Okay."

"Everybody's shocked and saddened about Joe," Tom said.

"Everybody except Gonzales."

"Yeah."

The two men spoke in low tones for a few more minutes. When the waitress arrived with the dinners, Tom excused himself.

Ashley watched Luke sit back down.

"I guess Gonzales gives you a lot of trouble?" she asked.

He shrugged.

"From my clients, I get the impression he's turned being a grade-A jerk into an art form."

Luke laughed. "Yeah."

She picked up a taco and took a bite, but wasn't feeling very hungry. Luke was also picking at his food.

"Joe made a big difference in my life. I'm going to miss him."

"Me, too."

He shifted in his seat. "I told you there were three of us hell-raisers. Tom was the other one. Now I'm the only one who isn't respectable."

"Of course you are!" Ashley answered, not sure why she felt the need to defend him.

"Gonzales doesn't think so."

"Gonzales isn't happy unless he's making someone else miserable."

They both went back to poking at their food.

"I have to find out what happened to Joe," Luke finally said.

"I don't think it's a good idea to get in Gonzales's way."

"I don't think I will. I'm going out tomorrow to look for the gun he thinks is a figment of my imagination."

"My imagination, too. I'm coming with you."

"You don't need to do that."

"I feel the same way you do about Joe. And I agree with you about Gonzales. He needs some help doing his job."

Luke shook his head. "Fine."

"Let me know what time I should be ready tomorrow."

"Six-thirty sharp," he answered immediately.

He wasn't going to discourage her by setting out at dawn.

"I can meet you out on the road to Black Canyon," she responded.

"No, I'll pick you up," he answered sharply, making it clear that he wasn't going to take no for an answer.

They rode in silence back to her apartment, but Ashley realized that she'd talked more to Luke Cordova in the past few hours than she had in two years. And she thought she understood him better. She knew that his father, Joe's brother, had also been a hell-raiser and that he'd died in a single-car accident when Luke had been a baby. Luke's mother had left the pueblo when her only son had been sentenced to prison.

But Joe had stood by Luke—thank God. And he'd done better than most men in Sena Pueblo.

Meanwhile, Ashley had grown up with parents who loved her, stood by her, helped her in every way they could. Her life couldn't be more different from Luke's, she thought as they pulled up to her place. Did that mean they could never be friends?

DESPITE HIS RESERVATIONS, Luke picked up Ashley right on schedule as he'd promised, and drove them out into the desert.

"I should have left you home," he said, voicing his concern. From the corner of his eye he saw that Ashley looked as tense as he felt.

"This is as important to me as it is to you," she snapped.

"Joe didn't save your life!" he shot back, then wished he hadn't put it in those terms.

"He was my connection to the pueblo. My real father, Brian Thompson, ran out on my mother. And she fled to Los Angeles. If Joe hadn't been here, I would have left a long time ago."

He might have told her that that would have been the best course. A woman who'd grown up in an upscale suburb of Los Angeles didn't belong working in a welfare office in Nowhere, New Mexico. But he wasn't going to start an argument. So he drove silently past the spot where they'd been ambushed and past the tire tracks where the cops had parked yesterday.

Yesterday.

It seemed like a thousand years ago when he'd found Joe's body.

He got out his pack, where he'd stuffed a pair of

thick leather gloves, then jammed a broad-brimmed hat onto his head and shouldered the coils of rope.

"What do you want me to do?" she asked.

Since she didn't have the sense to stay where she was safe, he reached into the glove compartment and removed the same gun he'd taken with him yesterday.

"Stand guard," he answered in a flat voice.

She accepted the weapon without hesitation. It flashed into his mind that Joe had taken her out into the desert for several shooting lessons and bragged about how well she'd done.

And she knew how to dress for this expedition. She was wearing jeans, a long-sleeved shirt and hiking boots for their outing. Even though the shirt was a little too tight-fitting for his comfort. He moved quickly to the edge of the rock face and she kept up with him. When she'd first arrived in New Mexico, she never would have been able to do it. It took a while for people to adjust to the high altitude. But she seemed to be in good shape, he thought with grudging admiration.

And she had another trait he liked, too. She didn't ask a bunch of questions. She didn't speak until they reached the top of the cliff. Stopping short, she pointed to the yellow crime scene tape tied to small survey flags. "Did you know that was there?" she asked.

"Yeah."

"But we can't…"

"There's nothing to say I can't move a few yards away and go over the edge."

"Okay," she murmured as she watched him tie the rope to a boulder, pull on his gloves and test his weight on the line.

The tension on her face was stark as he prepared to

go over the side and make the hundred-foot descent to the canyon floor. Finally she spoke. "Be careful."

"I intend to."

He lowered himself over the edge, then started down, bracing his feet against the cliff. About halfway down, a piece of the wall in front of him gave way and Ashley stared in horror as rock began crashing around him, raining down to the canyon floor.

Chapter Six

The rope in front of Ashley trembled. And the sound of rock tumbling into the canyon was like thunder booming out across the desert landscape.

She felt her heart stop then start up again in double time.

Her own scream added to the sound. "Luke! Luke! Are you all right?" she called, moving closer to the edge of the cliff, trying to see over the side.

A cloud of dust rose in her face, obscuring her vision, making her cough. From below, she heard more coughing.

"Luke?" she called again. "For God's sake, tell me you're all right."

"Mostly," came the strangled answer.

The rope shook as he hauled himself up rapidly. When she saw his head and shoulders appear, she set down the gun and reached over to pull him the rest of the way. They tumbled together onto the rocks, sending up a cloud of dust, but she could see that his hat had saved his head and face from the worst of the rockfall.

"What happened?" she breathed raggedly.

"A section of the wall gave way under my foot. Then stuff from above tumbled down, too."

He was in her arms, but an image had lodged in her

mind—an image of Luke falling to the floor of the canyon.

Even though he was alive and safe, she needed to express the gratitude coursing through her.

She angled her head, bringing her lips down on his. Maybe she meant it as a quick kiss—a way to show her relief—but once she connected, something hot and electric flared between them.

Perhaps his brush with death had made him reach for life. All she knew was that his hold on her turned possessive. And his mouth opened against hers so that he could devour her with his lips, his tongue, his teeth.

She kissed him back with the same passion. Her head spun as her mouth moved against his, her hands stroking up and down his back.

She'd been reserved around him. Shy even. But control evaporated like water on scorching rocks.

And the man in her arms seemed willing—no, eager—to take anything she wanted to give. When his embrace tightened around her, she heard him groan.

One of his hands tangled in her hair and cupped the back of her head, holding her mouth where he wanted it. The other slipped down her body, pulling her hips against his, so that she could feel his response to her. The intimate contact sent shock waves over her fiery skin.

He rolled onto his back, taking her with him so that she was sprawled on top of his body, her middle pressed to his.

"Ah, *chiquita.*"

He held her tightly, passionately, tenderly. But as he moved his leg, his foot must have hit a small rock because she heard it tumble over the edge, then crash to the canyon floor far below.

She felt his whole body tense. In the next second he

set her away from him as he sat up and uttered a low curse, then added, "Sorry! I was completely out of line."

She wanted to look away in embarrassment. But she kept her gaze steady on him.

"You don't have anything to apologize for," she said as she brushed dust from her clothing. "I was scared for you. Then when you came back over the edge of the cliff, I—I was so relieved that I grabbed you. So if it's anyone's fault, it's mine," she added, struggling to be perfectly clear when her thoughts were whirling around in her head like a tornado.

She wasn't lying. She had been worried. And she had grabbed him. But she hadn't been prepared for what happened after that. She got the feeling that neither had he.

He looked away, over the edge of the cliff. "I should try again," he muttered.

"To go down there?"

"Yeah."

Her response was a panicked, "No! I almost had a heart attack when those rocks fell." She heaved in a breath and let it out. "I guess the police are right about the face of the cliff being unstable."

He nodded. "Or somebody made it that way."

"What does that mean?"

"If somebody wanted to keep people from going down, they could loosen some of the rocks."

"Who would do that? And how?"

"A witch could do it."

They were back to witches, and she didn't want to go there again. Really, she didn't want to think that supernatural forces were interfering in her life. But was that worse than thinking that Joe had lost his mind?

"You should get cleaned up," she said.

"I've been dirtier," he muttered.

"Well, it's not too far to your house, is it?" As soon as she'd asked the question, she wished she had left well enough alone. She shouldn't be inviting herself to his home.

"It's not too far," he allowed as he untied the rope, then picked up his pack while she collected the gun.

They drove back toward civilization, neither of them speaking. Obviously he was as embarrassed as she was. Now she wished she'd showed better control.

FRED GONZALES took a last drag on his cigarette, then crushed it out in the ashtray. Really, he would have liked to toss it onto the gravel of the parking area, but he'd learned to rein in some of his less socially acceptable impulses.

He got out of his SUV and stretched, looking up at the back of the art gallery. It was a very nice building. High-class. Designed as a tourist trap. Rico Tafoya did pretty well here—considering where he'd come from.

He snorted. Of course, he had a good idea where Rico had gotten the money to open the gallery.

Pushing away from the cruiser, he walked up the steps to the front door. Really, the FBI had jurisdiction over any murder at the pueblo. But he hated calling them in. And never more than with this case.

Once inside, he stopped, soaking up the high-priced atmosphere. Not much like the little homes where most of the Sena people lived.

Tafoya stepped around the corner and his expression darkened.

Fred stood where he was, enjoying the feeling of power. All people had to do was to see his uniform and they got a little jolt of fear. That was because everybody had something to hide. Everybody had stuff they wanted to keep secret.

When Fred didn't speak, Tafoya was forced to ask, "Something I can do for you?"

"I'd like your cooperation in a murder investigation."

"I'd cooperate…if I knew anything."

Fred didn't like his attitude. "You can tell me who bought several of Joe's paintings at the beginning of the show."

"I could, if the buyer hadn't asked me to keep the sales confidential."

"Stop playing games and tell me who bought those paintings. Unless you want some trouble."

WHEN THE MOTION of the car changed, Ashley looked through the windshield and breathed out an appreciative sigh. They were on a long private drive that led up to a low adobe house built in the traditional style and nestled beneath a magnificent backdrop of red rocks and cloud-streaked sky.

The house was framed by cottonwood, box elders and piñons. Along the parking area, raised beds held an assortment of drought-resistant plants—mock heather, rabbitbrush and low, decorative cacti.

She followed Luke up a flagstone path, feeling a sense of anticipation, knowing the interior would reflect his personality. He unlocked the door and they stepped into a peaceful environment that blended the best of old and new traditions. Shelves holding books and pottery and baskets were built into the thick walls. A kiva fireplace filled one corner. Grouped around it, resting on a bold red-and-black rug, were low Barcelona chairs.

"This room is beautiful," she said, thinking that it was

warm and comfortable and very much anchored to the Southwest.

"It suits me," he answered, then gestured down a short hallway. "There's a guest bathroom on the right. You might want to wash up. I'll be back in a few minutes."

She hadn't thought about how she might look. Now she hurried into the bathroom and peered into the mirror, seeing that she was indeed the worse for wear. The best she could do was to run a comb through her hair, then pull off her shirt to do a decent job of cleaning up.

After a quick wash, she stared at her reflection, her gaze focused on her lips. They looked swollen, very thoroughly kissed. She saw her cheeks color as she remembered the heated scene after Luke had made it to the top of the cliff.

She'd reached for him, clung to him. But the emotions hadn't been one-sided. His response to her had been just as strong. Or at least, it seemed that way to her.

So where did they go from here? Or was the kiss an aberration that would not be repeated?

As she stood there, half-dressed, her cell phone rang and she dug it out of her purse.

Anita Morales, the young woman who had needed an emergency appendectomy, was on the other end of the line. Ashley knew she should be at the casino—where she worked as a maid.

"Anita, is there some problem?" she asked.

"No. No. I'm good. I'm sorry to call you on the cell phone."

"That's fine."

"I'm taking a break and I wanted to give you some information. About Joe."

"Yes?"

"You know they keep some of the offices in the back

locked. Well, I was passing the door when Miguel came out." Miguel Silva was the casino manager.

"Inside I saw one of Joe's paintings. You'd think they'd want to show it off. But it was locked up. Maybe you should find out why."

"Thank you for telling me, Anita."

"I gotta go."

"Wait—give me your number."

Anita spit it out, then the line went dead. Quickly Ashley pulled a pen from her purse and scribbled down the number on the back of an old sales slip.

A knock at the door made her jump. "Is everything okay?"

"I don't know. Wait a minute." Quickly she put down the phone, pulled on her shirt and buttoned it before opening the door.

Luke was standing in the hallway, wearing fresh jeans and a T-shirt, his hair still wet from the shower. When his gaze drilled into her chest, she looked down and saw that in her haste she'd buttoned her shirt wrong.

She quickly fixed it, then said awkwardly, "That was one of my clients. Anita Morales. She works as a maid at the casino, and she says that one of Joe's paintings is locked up in an office there."

He wedged his hands on his hips. "If it's locked up, how does she know?"

"I asked her that. She got a look at it when Miguel Silva came out. She says she recognized Joe's style."

"She could be wrong about the artist."

"Yes."

He sighed. "If it's Joe's, I want to find out what it's doing there."

She was waiting for him to say that they didn't have

to go together. Apparently he realized that dismissing her out of hand was no longer an option.

Did that mean something between them had changed? Or had he simply wanted to avoid a fight?

AS THEY HEADED for the casino, she turned to Luke. "You have to make sure that Anita doesn't get into trouble. I mean, you can't tell Miguel that she's the one who called me about the painting."

"Understood."

Ten minutes later they pulled into the large parking lot next to the casino.

The facility was near the shopping center that served the pueblo and surrounding areas, but it sat a little apart from the commercial area.

The building was massive, a strange combination of modern and traditional, with a massive porch held up by huge hewn logs that spanned the front of the beige stone facade.

Banks of double doors welcomed gamblers. As she and Luke stepped inside and onto the thick carpet, Ashley was assaulted by the jingle of slot machines—even though it was still morning. Apparently time had no meaning in the perpetual twilight of the casino.

Looking into the gambling area, she spotted several of her clients sitting at the machines and had to stifle the impulse to march across the room to yank Enrique Ramos out of his seat. He could barely support his family. But here he was wagering his paycheck. She pressed her lips together and watched Luke step up to one of the floor managers.

"Help you?" the man asked.

"Luke Cordova, Ashley Donaldson. We'd like to speak to Miguel."

"Mr. Silva?"

"Yes."

He turned his head toward a shirt-collar microphone, pressed a button and spoke into it. When he received an answer, he walked to a door, pressed in a key code, then opened the door.

"Down that hall, to the reception area."

They walked into the back of the house, which was every bit as opulent as the public area. A cute blonde who obviously didn't come from the pueblo sat behind a wide wooden desk.

"Just a moment," she said.

She picked up a phone, dialed a number, then announced their presence.

A moment later Miguel Silva stepped out of an office to their right and ushered them inside. He was a heavy man in his fifties, dressed in dark slacks, a white shirt and a checkered sports coat. The hair on the top of his head was thinning. To compensate, he wore a long ponytail that Ashley thought looked ridiculous.

"Sorry to hear about your loss," he said to Luke.

"Thanks."

"What can I do for you?"

"We've heard that one of Joe's paintings had turned up here."

"Heard from whom?"

"Word gets around," Luke answered.

"It's got to be one of my employees," Silva muttered, making Ashley cringe.

"No. It was someone from my work crew," Luke answered, straight-faced.

"Casino property is certainly none of your business."

"Did somebody use it to settle a gambling debt?" Luke asked.

"I can't comment."

When Luke looked as though he was going to charge down the hall and start opening doors, Ashley put a restraining hand on his arm. He swung toward her, his face angry.

She looked at Silva. "Do you take merchandise for gambling debts?"

"We don't discuss our business practices."

"As you can imagine, we're very upset about Joe's death. We're trying to find out what happened to him," she murmured. "Now that he's dead, his paintings will immediately go up in price. Whoever killed him would know that."

Silva's expression softened. "I understand. And I'm sorry. But we can't break the confidence of our patrons."

"So it was a patron," she said.

"I was just speaking figuratively."

She heard Luke make a snorting sound. "Come on."

When he turned and marched down the hall, she followed. As they stepped into the public area of the casino, he muttered a curse.

"Everything here is recorded," she reminded him softly.

"Right."

He waited until they'd stepped outside before saying, "We shouldn't have come. He wouldn't tell us a damn thing!"

"But we know from his answers that he's got the picture." She gave him an appreciative look. "That was fast thinking about your work crew."

"Yeah. I had a licensed electrician and some of my men working here. I assume Silva isn't going to call us again."

"Oh—I'm sorry."

"Don't worry about it," he snapped.

But she realized that charging over here had probably cost him a very lucrative account.

They reached the SUV and climbed in. She wanted to ask what they should do now, but she remained silent. Until a few days ago, she'd thought she understood exactly where she stood with Luke Cordova—less than nowhere. Now she was having confusing thoughts about him that she should repress. Because there could be no future for the two of them. Grief had brought them together. But that was hardly enough to sustain a relationship.

"Why don't we pick up my car," she murmured. "Then I can go back to work."

"Fine," he snapped, and she was left with the feeling that she had somehow played it wrong again.

They drove silently back to Luke's house. But when they pulled into the parking area, a battered pickup was sitting beside Ashley's car. As Luke cut the engine, Tom Lahi climbed out and ran a hand through his short, dark hair. He looked unsettled. And he also didn't look pleased to see Ashley.

Chapter Seven

Maybe she was overreacting, Ashley thought as she climbed out of the SUV. But she was tired of having men messing with her. Luke Cordova. Miguel Silva. Fred Gonzales. And now it looked as though Tom was in the same mood as all the other guys.

She'd thought of him as a friend. Now he gave her a closed look. "Luke and I have some private business to discuss."

"If it's about Joe, it's not private," she said angrily. "I care as much about Joe as he does."

Luke gave a small shrug. "Whatever you have to say, you can say it in front of her."

"Are you sure?" Tom asked, his tone making it clear that he didn't agree.

"Yeah. I'm perfectly sure," Luke allowed.

"Okay. I picked up some information from the 'desert drums' and went to Rico for confirmation."

"And?" Luke prompted.

"And Rico told me you bought a bunch of Joe's paintings right before the show."

Ashley sucked in a breath but managed to keep silent.

"What about it?" Luke asked.

"Gonzales knows about it. He's moved you to the top of his murder suspect list."

Luke's eyes turned hard.

Before he could answer, Ashley heard herself saying, "He and I spent the night together—after Joe failed to show up at the gallery."

Tom's gaze shot to her and she felt her face heat when she realized that her subconscious had started speaking before her mind was engaged.

"I—I mean, Luke has an alibi. We spent the night together in Joe's house—sitting in the family room, waiting for him to come back. Then in the morning, we went together to look for him. So...so I was with him the whole time."

"You're sure about that? The whole time?" Tom said, grilling her as though she were on the witness stand.

She felt her chest tighten as she remembered exactly what had happened.

Luke jumped into the conversation. "Actually, she wasn't with me every second. She fell asleep on the couch."

"Raul Estevez stopped by," Ashley interjected. "He saw us together in the morning. Before Joe was killed. At least, I think it was before," she added lamely. "Luke and I were making assumptions."

"There's one more factor you'd better add in," Luke went on, as though she hadn't spoken. "Later, when we went up toward Black Canyon to look for Joe, someone started shooting at us—"

"I didn't hear about that," Tom interjected.

"Yeah, well, I suppose Gonzales isn't talking about it."

"Okay. What exactly happened?"

"I pulled to the side of the road and got Ashley into the ditch," Luke answered. "Then I grabbed my gun and tried to circle around in back of the sniper. We heard one last shot. We figured that's when Joe died."

"Did you discharge your weapon?" Tom asked Luke.

"No."

"You should have asked for a gunpowder residue test."

"I guess it's too late for that now," Luke answered.

"When you're dealing with the police, you have to be honest about the details. Or you can get into trouble."

Luke laughed, and it wasn't a nice sound. "That's a little difficult concept for someone like me. If you recall, I tried being honest a long time ago. It didn't do me any good. You can't count on being saved because you're innocent."

Tom reached out a hand, clasped Luke's shoulder, then dropped his hand to his side again. "I shouldn't be lecturing you."

"I appreciate the warning about Gonzales."

"Can you tell me why you bought the paintings?" Tom asked.

Luke shifted his weight from one foot to the other. "I guess it doesn't make any difference now. Joe was acting worried about something. And he wouldn't talk to me about it. He was a proud man."

"Yes," Ashley whispered.

"I decided that if it was money problems, I could do something about that. So I arranged to buy five of his paintings—at the price he was asking before the show started."

"And Gonzales found out," Ashley whispered. "He knows the paintings are a lot more valuable now than they were before Joe died."

Tom took a step back. "I just wanted you to know what was going on in the investigation."

"And you wanted to find out why I'd bought a bunch of artwork," Luke added.

"I knew you had a good reason," his friend answered.

"I appreciate your coming by," Luke said, sounding as though he didn't really mean it.

Tom climbed back into his truck and backed down the drive. Ashley watched him go, then looked at Luke. His features had turned rigid. "I am not going back into a jail cell," he said in a voice as sharp as blades tearing into ice.

As Tom had done, she reached out to touch him. "Don't…" She was going to say, "Do anything stupid." But this time her brain was working and the advice choked off before it reached her lips. Instead she said, "I care about what happens to you."

"That's probably a mistake," he clipped out.

Wordlessly, she clasped her arms around him. His already taut muscles went even tighter. Before he could jerk away from her, she let go and walked away, getting her purse from his car and heading for her vehicle. All without saying a single word to the man she'd suddenly, dangerously, started to feel too much for.

THE PUEBLO was obviously a very tight-knit society. By the next day, she found out that Luke had arranged for Joe's funeral on Friday—two days away. The funeral was at a church in Santa Fe, because it was larger than anything closer to the pueblo.

Ashley sat in the back of the Santa Fe church, silently gratified that so many people had turned out for Joe's funeral.

And she was surprised to hear some of the things people said about him. Apparently he hadn't exactly been an upstanding citizen in his youth. It sounded as though he'd been as wild as Luke. Then a high school teacher who thought Joe'd had talent had submitted some of his works to a local art school. He'd gotten a scholarship, which had changed his life. But he'd never forgotten that he was part of the Sena community.

She hadn't seen Luke in almost three days. He was seated in the front of the church. He wasn't one of the people who spoke, though she saw many friends of his and Joe's coming up to him and offering their condolences. She wasn't one of them. She had come to the sad conclusion that making any kind of overture toward him was a waste of time.

After the church service they went outside and the men from the pueblo performed a traditional funeral dance. Women had set up a feast, but Ashley had trouble choking down any food.

Just as she was about to leave, a gray-haired man in a dark suit walked up to her. "Ms. Donaldson?"

"Yes."

"I'm sorry to meet you under these circumstances. But I'm Bill Laredo, Joe Cordova's lawyer."

He stuck out his hand and she shook it.

"What can I do for you?" she asked.

"Joe mentioned you in his will. I'd like to make an appointment to discuss the bequest."

She stared at him. "He left something to *me?*"

"Yes. He changed his will a year ago. We should talk about it in my office." He handed her a card, which she stuffed into her purse. She hadn't expected anything like this; it made his death even more of a reality.

Joe had been her connection to the pueblo. With her good friend gone, she was wondering why she was hanging around New Mexico. She had tried to fit in, but she had never quite made it. Maybe it was time to go back to Los Angeles.

SHE WAS TOUCHED that Joe had mentioned her in his will. Still, she put off calling the lawyer because she simply couldn't deal with such final proof that he was gone. But the subject of the artist came up again two days later when one of her clients came up to her in the grocery store parking lot.

After looking around to make sure nobody was listening, Serena Tomoso whispered, "Joe's ghost is haunting his house."

Ashley struggled to hide her surprise. "What makes you think so?"

"People are talking about it. Sometimes lights go on and off. But there are no cars up there."

"It could be his nephew. He has to empty the house and get it ready for sale."

"Then where's his truck?" the woman challenged. Before Ashley could answer, Serena hurried on, "There are other things, too."

"Like what?"

"The coyote howls."

"But there are coyotes in the desert," Ashley answered. "Don't they always howl?"

"Maybe you don't believe because you don't come from here," the woman said.

The accusation stung. Another reminder that she was an outsider. "I do come from here," she said softly.

She had stopped at the grocery on her way home from the office. Now, instead of going home, she headed in the other direction—toward Joe's house.

She wasn't sure why she was going there. To prove she believed in ghosts—because that would make her a real daughter of the pueblo? To prove there were no ghosts? To give herself an opportunity to bump into Luke, since they hadn't spoken in days?

It was twilight by the time she took the turnoff to Joe's property. As she approached the house, she saw no lights inside—although the lamp by the front door was lit. There was a vehicle in the driveway. But it looked like Joe's SUV. The one he'd bought a few months ago.

Pulling onto the parking pad, she cut her engine, then got out, feeling the isolation of the area.

Maybe this was a dumb idea? Maybe she should have waited until morning.

But this was Joe's house. She'd been here often. She wasn't going to run away now. The least she could do was make sure the door was locked.

Still she fought an unsettled feeling as she walked through the darkness toward the light beside the front door. The blackness of the desert night seemed to press in around her. And the closer she got to the house, the more her steps slowed.

Finally she decided that she'd made a mistake by coming here. Just as she turned to leave, a coyote howled in the darkness. It sounded too close for comfort—raising the hairs on the back of her neck.

She whirled and made a dash for the car. But as she sprinted down the front walk, the air above her came alive with the beating of huge wings. In the next moment, a giant bird dove out of the sky toward her. At least, it sounded like a bird, although she could see nothing. But all her other senses shrieked danger.

A wing slapped against her face.

Screaming, she ducked her head. Eyes closed, she bent at the knees and covered her hair with her arms as the bird flapped around her.

Over the sound of beating wings, she heard tires squeal, a door slam.

The bird screeched, its call high and angry. Then it flapped away.

Seconds later someone shouted and she whirled toward the source of the exclamation.

Scuffling noises came from her right but the side of the house blocked her line of sight. Running to the corner of the house, she peered into the darkness and thought she made out two men fighting. One of the men got in a blow with a heavy object before running off into the desert.

A loud curse rang out as the man on the ground scrambled up and ran in hot pursuit after the escapee.

She recognized the voice. It was Luke.

But both he and the other man had vanished into the desert.

Out in the darkness, he cursed again. Then in the background she heard the sound of an engine turning over.

Her heart leaped into her throat. "Luke?" she called. "Luke. Are you all right?"

Chapter Eight

Luke wanted to simply fade into the darkness. But Ashley was here, so he walked toward her, trying not to limp.

"What happened?" she gasped.

Yeah. What?

He settled for, "The bastard hit me with a flashlight, I think. Something hard anyway."

He was trying to stand straight. But when he wavered on his feet, she took his arm. "Come inside and let me see."

He resisted the impulse to wrench away. Letting her steer him toward the door, he waited while she fumbled to find the key.

Finally she got it in the lock. After opening the door, she turned on the light in the front hall, making them both blink.

Seconds later he heard her distressed sound.

"What?"

"He hurt you," she gasped.

"The bastard got away!"

"Who?"

"I'd like to know." Pushing past her, he hurried down the hall to the bathroom and snapped on the overhead fixture.

When he bent and peered into the mirror, he swore.

Ashley stared at his reflection in apparent horror.

"It's not so bad," he assured her as he reached toward the big red gouge on his cheek.

She snatched his hand away. "Let me clean it."

She opened the linen closet, grabbed a washcloth and wet it under the hot water. Then she added soap and carefully dabbed at the wound. It felt strange letting her fuss over him—especially since he felt like a jerk for allowing the guy to escape.

"Thanks," he muttered when she was finished.

"You should have that checked in the emergency room," she advised.

"No way." He grabbed a towel from the linen closet, then charged down the hall to the kitchen. Without turning on any more lights, he opened the freezer, snatched up some ice cubes and wrapped them in the towel.

Dropping onto the couch, he leaned his head back and closed his eyes as he held the towel against his cheek.

Not looking at her didn't make him feel any better.

"What happened?" she asked.

"I saw you turn off onto the road to Joe's."

"You knew it was me?"

"Yeah. So I followed you. What are you doing up here?" he asked, glad to take the focus off his screwup.

"One of my clients said that…that—" She stopped and gulped. "That Joe's ghost was haunting the house. I don't know if I wanted to prove it wasn't true—or if I wanted to take an excursion into pueblo traditions."

"And?"

"Before you came, I heard the coyote. And…"

"What?" he demanded.

"The bird dived at me. It was flapping around my head."

He swore.

"What was it?"

"I'd like to know!"

"A witch?"

"Whoever hit me did it in the conventional way."

They were both silent for several heartbeats.

"How does your face feel?" she finally asked.

"Fine!"

"Are you getting mad at me again?" she asked in a hurt voice.

"I'm not mad at you!"

"Then why are you so…uptight and angry?" she asked with a bluntness that made him wince.

"I'm mad at myself for letting that guy whack me and escape."

"He saw you coming. I mean, he must have been here when I arrived." She got up and crossed the room to stand in front of him. "So don't beat yourself up. Think about it this way—you probably saved my life."

He couldn't argue with that part. His heart had literally stopped when he'd seen her standing in front of Joe's house, being attacked by something that seemed to be invisible. He didn't know what had happened. All he knew was that keeping her at a distance was suddenly not an option.

He stood, set the ice pack on the glass-topped side table, then reached for Ashley.

Giving her time to pull away, he drew her slowly into his arms. She came willingly, ending up with her head on his shoulder and her arms around his waist.

He trailed his hand through her hair. Such lovely brown hair. His other hand stroked up and down her strong back.

Just touching her was a wonderful luxury. The effect on him was profound. He was instantly aroused, although he wasn't going to do anything about that unless he knew she wanted it.

But he knew she could feel his erection. Knew by the way her stance changed.

"Luke?"

Hardly able to catch his breath, he managed to say, "I can take you back to your car. And you can get out of here."

"I hope not," she answered, then raised her face. His lips met hers in the sweetest kiss he had ever experienced. And at the same time, the most potent.

His only reality was the irresistible woman he held in his arms. His heart slammed against the inside of his chest as he drank from her, gathered her into a tighter embrace.

They swayed together and he moved his head back and forth, sliding his mouth against hers. Did she feel the way he did—on the edge and unable to stop himself from falling into space?

Since the first time he had met her, he had wanted Ashley Donaldson. Now that she was in his arms, he wanted to experience her every way he could. Reaching to the side, he switched on the table lamp, then looked down into her startled face.

"I have to see you," he growled.

"I'm nothing special."

He couldn't hold back his shock. "You think that?"

"I think I got the worst of my father's and my mother's heritage."

He cupped his hand around the back of her head, ran his finger along her feathery brows, traced her generous lower lip, stroked her delicate jaw. "You are so…so wrong. You got the best…the very best, *chiquita.*"

"No…"

"You don't know when to keep your mouth shut," he said before stopping her words with his own mouth. He kissed her thoroughly while he reached around to slip his hands under her knit top and open the catch of her bra. Then he brought his hands back around, cradling her breasts, stroking his thumbs across the crests.

She moaned into his mouth, her response leaving him shaking. He didn't want to break the kiss, but it was the only way he could pull her shirt up and over her head, bringing the bra with it, leaving her naked to the waist.

He reached to touch her again. "Beautiful, so beautiful," he murmured.

Around her neck was a thick silver chain. Hanging from it, dipping between her breasts, was a flat, silver disk studded with a light green turquoise. He touched it with his finger. The workmanship was beautiful. "What is this?"

She looked down. "It's the only thing I have left from my father. He gave it to my mother before he disappeared."

"Oh."

Then, as though she were changing the subject, she reached for the hem of his T-shirt and tugged it up. He helped her, tearing the shirt off before pulling her back into his arms, the sensation of his hot skin against hers making them both drag in a sharp breath.

"Luke. Oh, Luke," she gasped.

HE COULD HARDLY believe he was standing here, with Ashley Donaldson naked in his arms. He ached to make love with her—and to make it good for her.

"Come on." Linking his hand with hers, he led her down the hall to the guest room they had both slept in—at different times, of course, although he'd thought about her being there.

Maybe he was giving her time to regain her sanity and to get out of the house. But she came back to him just as willingly as she'd first stepped into his arms.

She was so sweet. So much more innocent than he was. He knew because it was easy to keep track of someone's social life in the closed society of the pueblo. And he knew she had dated only casually since she'd come here.

She'd stayed away from meaningful relationships. Yet she was with him now, and when she kissed him, it was like springtime and Christmas and coming home after being locked away.

His hands went to the hook at the top of her slacks. She let him unfasten them, then helped slick the garment down her legs, along with her panties.

His hands stroked over her back, her bottom, between her legs. And when he found her hot and wet and ready for him, his heart leaped.

He felt her fumbling with his belt buckle and closed his eyes, enjoying the sensation of her fingers moving against him. He kissed her ear, her neck, her shoulders while she dispatched the belt buckle, then opened the snap at the top of his jeans and lowered his zipper with a hand that wasn't quite steady. As she had done, he got rid of the jeans and his briefs quickly.

Again, the touch of his naked flesh against hers gave him a jolt; he heard her matching indrawn breath.

"I love your hair. Can I loosen it?" she whispered.

"Yes, *chiquita*. Anything you want."

Her hands went to the back of his neck, working at the band that held his ponytail in place. When she'd pulled it off, she combed her fingers through his hair, the intimacy of the gesture making his throat tighten.

He reached to pull the sheet and spread out of the way, then brought her with him to the surface of the bed, holding her and stroking her and kissing her. He had dreamed of this. He had never thought that dream would come true.

Yet she was in his arms. Naked. On a bed. Touching

him and kissing him with such openness and warmth that he felt his heart turn over.

"Luke...I need..."

The same thing he needed. But he kept his own desires in check as he took her higher and higher, his lips moving over her face and neck and breasts, his hand stroking and caressing to intensify her pleasure.

"Please...now...please," she gasped, closing her hand around his erection.

That intimate contact was almost more than he could endure.

He rolled her onto her back and rose over her, letting her guide him to her body before he plunged into her, claimed her.

"Oh, Luke."

"*Chiquita.* My beautiful *chiquita.*" Still stunned by this intimacy, he looked into her upturned face as he began to move.

He tried to keep the pace slow. But she told him wordlessly that she didn't want slow. She was as close to the edge as he was himself.

And as he felt his climax gather, he heard her cry out in ecstasy.

He drank in those glad cries as the power of the moment grabbed them, then swept them into a great wave of fulfillment.

Ashley clung to him, gasping for breath. When he could think coherently, he moved to his side, cradling her in his arms, too overwhelmed to do more than hold her.

"Thank you," she whispered. "Thank you for trusting me."

He wasn't sure what she meant, so he kissed her cheek.

She snuggled beside him and he stroked her hair, her shoulder.

The past few days had taken their toll on him and he drifted into sleep, still cradling her body against his.

HE WOKE when the sun streamed in around the sides of the blinds. For a panicked second he didn't know where he was. Then the incredible events of the night came back to him.

Turning his head, he found Ashley lying close beside him, her eyes open.

"How does your cheek feel?" she asked.

"Okay." He shifted. The morning after had never been awkward for him, but he felt awkward now. Maybe that was why he heard himself ask, "Are you sorry about making love with me?"

"No, but I'm guessing you are," she answered.

"It shouldn't have happened."

"I don't agree." She sighed. "But I'm not going to argue with you about it. And I'm not going to let you make me feel guilty, either. When you're ready to accept what happened, we can talk about it."

"What would you say if we were ready to talk?" he managed.

"That you and I care about each other. That Joe's death made it possible for us to…connect. But you're not willing to admit it yet."

He opened his mouth, then realized he didn't know what he wanted to say. So he closed his lips again as he watched her climb out of bed, hurry to the bureau and take out clean clothing, which she held in front of herself when she turned back to him.

"In case you don't remember, it's Saturday. So neither one of us is late for work." After delivering that statement, she disappeared into the bathroom. Moments later he heard the shower running.

He didn't want to be in bed, naked, when she emerged fully dressed. So he got up, collected his scattered clothing and headed for one of the other bathrooms.

When he came out, he couldn't find her, and for a panicked moment, he thought she'd left. Then he heard her cry out and went running down the hall to the art studio—cursing the lack of a weapon.

Chapter Nine

Ashley whirled around as Luke came charging through the door, barefoot and defenseless, his wet hair hanging around his face and his features making him look like an ancient warrior.

He glanced wildly around the room as though he expected to confront an invader. "What happened?"

She gestured toward the paintings that he'd lined up along the wall several days earlier.

Open tubes of paint lay on the floor, along with a putty knife, and he saw at once that someone had come in here and slashed streaks of paint across the canvases.

"Someone ruined them!"

She put a hand on his arm. When she felt his muscles harden, she pulled her fingers back. "Maybe not. I took an art history class at UCLA. One thing they talked about was restoring old paintings. They can bring back the work of a Renaissance master. And there's a better chance here because it takes a long time for oil paint to dry."

"I hope you're right."

"Why would someone slash paint across Joe's work?"

He shrugged. "Maybe he's trying to keep us from figuring out what's in those pictures."

"Like what?"

"I don't know!"

"Didn't Joe sometimes work from photographs?" she asked.

"Yeah. Let's try to find some."

She was glad to have a job to focus on as she began opening desk drawers—and he searched through the cluttered shelves that lined one wall. Finally Luke called, "I think I've found them."

Ashley hurried to his side. He was holding a battered accordion folder that was stuffed with old photos.

He handed her some pictures and she shuffled through them. Many were of the same areas that were in the paintings. But she couldn't tell by looking at the photographs what was important enough to cover up.

"We should go down to the gallery and make sure nobody has harmed the paintings there," Luke said.

Ashley pressed her hand against her mouth. "I should have thought of that."

"I didn't until just now."

He tucked the folder under his arm, then strode out of the room. Ashley followed and found him standing in the family room.

"Do you mind leaving your car and picking it up later?" he asked.

"Why?"

"So it looks like the house is occupied."

"That will work, unless someone is watching the place now."

"There's not much cover during daylight in the desert. I assume we're safe until the evening."

She nodded, then followed him to his SUV. She wanted to ask what he was thinking about the two of them. But she'd long ago learned that Luke Cordova didn't speak his mind until he was good and ready.

So they rode in silence toward Santa Fe. To her embarrassment, she heard her stomach growl.

When they reached the outskirts of town, he pulled into the drive-thru of a fast-food restaurant. "What do you want?"

"An egg and sausage sandwich, I guess. And some coffee with cream and sugar."

He put in two identical orders, except that he asked for his coffee black.

They ate as they drove the rest of the way to the gallery, and she had never felt more separated from another human being. Last night he'd seemed like he cared about her. This morning, he had walled himself off again.

So what was between them? Just sex?

She didn't believe that was true. But she'd already told him what she thought. And he was acting as though they'd only shaken hands last night....

The familiar flute and acoustic guitar music was playing in the background when they entered the gallery. By silent agreement, they headed toward the room where Joe's paintings were displayed—and found Charlotte Reyna looking upset.

Ashley crossed to her. "Charlotte, what happened?"

She looked up, shook her head.

"Can you tell us?" Ashley pressed.

"There was something…about the painting."

"Let's sit down," Ashley said. As they settled in the chairs in the corner, some of the photos Luke was carrying fell out of the folder.

Charlotte stared down at them. "Where did you get those?"

"They were in Joe's studio," Ashley answered. "After he died, someone used a putty knife to slap paint on some of his paintings."

Charlotte gasped. "That's horrible."

"Do you know something about it?" Luke asked sharply.

Her features contorted. "No!"

Rapid footsteps made them all look up.

A door slammed and Rico rushed in. "What's going on?"

"Someone vandalized a dozen of Joe's paintings," Luke answered, watching his face.

Rico's horrified gaze shot to the works on the wall.

"Not these," Luke told him. "The ones that are still at his house. So you may want to lock these up."

When they turned back to Charlotte, she had scooped up the photographs and was shuffling through them.

"Do you see anything we should know about?" Ashley asked gently.

"Pottery."

"Where?"

She pointed to the lower right hand corner of a photograph.

"That looks like rocks," Ashley said.

"No…. I saw those paintings. It's broken pottery."

"Do you know something more about this?" Luke asked.

"No!" she repeated. "And please stop acting like I did something wrong."

"We're not," Ashley said. When Luke gave her a tense look, she steered him into the hall.

"She knows something," he growled.

"I…agree," Ashley admitted. "Maybe something happened when Rico was gone—and she's afraid to talk about it. Maybe he can get it out of her."

His gaze shot to the other couple. Rico was sitting beside Charlotte and they were talking quietly.

Luke dragged in a breath and let it out. "Okay, I won't ask her any more inconvenient questions. But I'm going back to the spot where Joe was murdered."

"Why?"

"Because I want to find that gun."

She wasn't sure that was possible. But at the same time, she wasn't going to let him go back to the scene of the crime alone.

"Then I'm going with you," she said.

"Why?"

"Because I think if you're going out there, you need somebody to watch your back."

He looked as though he was going to object. Then he gave an almost imperceptible nod.

Again, the silence in the car was palpable as they headed toward Black Canyon. Finally, Luke shifted in his seat. "Did you talk to Joe's lawyer?"

Her head swung toward him. "He came up to me after the funeral."

"And then?"

"He told me to make an appointment, but I haven't done it."

He shot her a surprised look, then focused on the road again. "Why?"

"Because I'm not sure whether I'm going to stay here," she blurted.

His foot bounced on the gas pedal. "Why not?"

"If there's nothing here for me, why stay?"

He cursed under his breath. "Are you trying to get me to say something I shouldn't say?"

Shock registered on her face. "No!"

"Then what?"

"I'm telling you how I feel," she answered simply.

His jaw went taut. "This is a bad time to get into a serious discussion."

"You asked a question. I answered it," she snapped.

They were almost to the place where someone had shot at them. Luke was obviously thinking about it, because he slowed, his eyes scanning the landscape.

When he pulled to an abrupt stop, she looked around in alarm. "What is it?"

"Get down."

"Another shooter?"

"Get down," he barked, and she unhooked her seat belt and slid off the seat.

Luke reached across and took the gun from the glove compartment. "Stay here," he ordered.

She didn't want to hide in the car while he went off to do something dangerous. "I'm calling the police," she said.

"No!"

"But…"

"If Gonzales shows up, I could end up with a bullet in the back."

She bit back a sharp response. For all she knew, he could be right. "At least tell me what you saw. And what are you going to do about it?"

"I saw somebody up on the ridge." He pointed to where they'd been a few days earlier. "And this time we have the advantage of surprise."

She wanted to ask him more questions. She wanted to keep him where he was and to let the police do their job. But she knew his instincts were correct—whoever was up there could disappear before help could arrive.

So she reached out to clasp Luke's shoulder when what she really wanted was to clasp him in her arms and keep him with her. "Be careful."

He gave her a long look. "I promise."

She loosened her hold, then watched him ease out of the SUV and slip through the rocks. But she knew that if something happened to him, she'd never forgive herself.

When he was out of sight, she carefully exited the car.

There were two ways up to the ridge—the one Luke had taken and another trail. Keeping low, she crept around the other side of the rocks, staying under cover as she climbed to the lip of the canyon.

At first she could see nothing, hear nothing.

Then the sound of a gunshot split the desert air—and her heart leaped into her throat.

Chapter Ten

Just as she had the last time, she ached to call out to Luke to make sure he was all right. But giving away her location was a dumb move. She had no weapon. No way to defend herself. Still, she kept moving. As she cautiously rounded an outcropping, she saw a man hiding behind a boulder. He was wearing a broad-brimmed hat and was holding a gun. He had it pointed away from her—in the direction of a large boulder. Behind it, she could see Luke crouched.

He spotted her as soon as her face peeked around the rock—and his features contorted.

She froze. Distracting him was the wrong thing to do.

The guy with the gun had spotted him and was moving from boulder to boulder, circling, trying to get into a better position.

She pointed, made a circling movement and knew from Luke's expression that he didn't understand the warning.

Quickly she bent, picked up a rock about the size of a football and held it over her head for several seconds. Then she heaved it as hard as she could to her left and ducked behind the protection of a rock.

The missile landed with a loud crash that broke the silence of the morning.

In response, the man with the gun whirled and fired.

Luke, who had watched her heave the stone, had already gotten closer to the shooter. Sprinting from cover, he came up behind the guy and knocked him to the ground, then kicked the weapon away before stepping back, his own weapon drawn.

"Put the gun down and raise your hands," he ordered.

The man hesitated for a moment, then slowly raised his hands, a look of despair on his face.

She gasped when she realized who it was. Roberto Sanchez, the janitor from the art gallery. The one whose sister had called about the painting hidden at the casino.

Ashley was almost too stunned to speak. But she managed to ask, "Did you kill Joe?"

"No! You have to believe me. I would never do something like that."

"Then what are you doing here?" she asked.

Roberto gave a quick shake of his head.

"He had Joe's gun." Luke spit the words out. He pointed to the familiar turquoise pattern inlaid into the handle. "Recognize it?"

"Yes."

"I—" Sanchez started to say, then closed his mouth.

"You have an explanation?" Luke asked.

"Let me go. I didn't do anything."

"Oh, sure. You're just out here looking for souvenirs from the murder scene. Too bad for you we came along at the wrong time." Luke fixed him with a dark stare. "Are you practicing witchcraft?"

"No!"

"What have you been doing out at Joe's house?"

"Nothing! It wasn't me."

"You can keep lying, but it won't do you any good," Luke muttered. Raising his head, he looked across at

Ashley, scowling. At that moment she was glad that a dozen feet and a deep chasm in the rocks separated them. He looked as though he wanted to throttle her. "I told you to stay in the car."

"It's a good thing I didn't," she shot back, then pulled the cell phone out of the purse that hung from her shoulder. It hadn't worked before when they were in this area, but maybe the higher elevation would make a difference. "I assume it's all right to call the cops—if I can get through."

"Yeah. Go ahead and try."

She dialed 9-1-1.

To her relief, the dispatcher came on the line.

Trying not to sound breathless, she explained why they needed police assistance and gave their location as well as she could.

Sanchez looked wildly around, as though he was desperate to make a break for it. She hated to think he was the one who had killed Joe, but she had no other choice.

When she heard sirens in the distance, she looked across at Luke. "I'm going down to meet the police."

"No, stay here!" he ordered. "I don't want any accidents."

She blanched. But she did as he asked. Half a minute later, she saw two policemen coming over the rise. Unfortunately one of them was Fred Gonzales, and she felt her heart start to pound, because she knew he wasn't going to believe a word Luke told him.

Trying for an end run, she started talking in a loud voice. "We're up here."

When the cops looked up, she continued quickly. "We found Robert Sanchez with Joe Cordova's gun. He shot at Luke. You can do a test to confirm that he fired his weapon—right? And to confirm that Luke hasn't."

"What are you, a lawyer?" Gonzales asked as he came closer.

"No. Just an informed citizen."

Sanchez had opened his mouth to speak. Apparently he thought better of saying anything.

Gonzales tipped his head to one side. "So how did you get the drop on him, Ms. Lawyer?"

"I was behind Roberto, where he couldn't see me. I threw a rock and distracted him," she answered. "And Luke was able to take the gun away. But if we need to discuss this in front of an attorney, I can call Tom Lahi."

"I think we can do this without a lawyer. I want the two of you to come in and make a statement. And I want to do gunpowder residue tests on both Luke and Roberto."

"Fine." Ashley climbed down from the rocks.

Gonzales immediately separated her and Luke—so that he could get their stories separately. When they arrived at the station, he questioned her first. Then Luke. Then he came back to her for more clarification.

Apparently he couldn't punch any holes in their stories. And Ashley was relieved to step into sunlight four hours later—with Luke at her side.

Clearing his throat, he asked, "Can we go back to my house and talk?"

Suddenly her chest was tight again. "About what?"

Luke looked back toward the grim facade of the police station. "I'd rather not start a conversation out here."

"Okay."

Or in the car, either, she discovered. So she endured another silent ride.

Quickly he led her through the door and into the cool, dark living room.

She watched him pace to the window, then turn back to face her. "I was pretty excited about cornering

Roberto. But the more I think about it, the more I wonder if it was really him."

"If he's innocent…"

"The law can still screw him!" Luke shouted. "So did we put an innocent man in jail?"

"We told Gonzalez what happened a few hours ago. Roberto sure wasn't innocent of trying to kill you!" Ashley said, her voice hard.

"Yeah, there's that." He scuffed his foot against the floorboards, then said, "I didn't ask you here to talk about Roberto."

"Then what?"

He huffed in a breath, then muttered, "You said you might leave New Mexico."

She felt her chest tighten. "Yes."

"You've done an amazing job at Pueblo Aid. Just like you did an amazing job with Gonzales. I felt like he'd caught me climbing in somebody's window. But you acted so cool and confident."

"Tom clued me in about how to handle Gonzales," she said, then asked, "How do you know about my track record at Pueblo Aid?"

"I hear a lot about the good work you're doing. People are always talking to me about you."

"Oh, they are?"

"Only good things."

"Well, I try to help my clients. But sometimes…I don't know if I'm making a dent."

"You are!" She watched him clench his hands, then slowly loosen them. "What if I asked you to stay? Would you?"

Her mouth was suddenly so dry that she had trouble speaking. "Why?"

The look on his face made her stomach knot. "Because I care about you."

Somehow she managed to ask, "Could you be a little more specific?"

He ran a hand through his hair, loosening some strands from his ponytail, then spoke almost under his breath. "Okay. I guess if you walk away from me, I won't be any worse off than I am now." He dragged in air and released it before saying. "I've been in love with you for a long time. I want you to stay here—with me."

She gasped. "In love with me?"

"Is that so strange?" he asked.

"Well, you were so distant. You acted like you didn't even like me."

"Because I thought you couldn't possibly be interested in a guy like me."

"You mean, a guy who started off with three strikes against him and completely turned his life around?" she answered.

"Joe…helped me."

"Sure he helped. He loved you. But you could have screwed up so badly. And you didn't. You are one of the biggest success stories around here. And I admired that so much. I wanted to be friends with you. Then I—I wanted to be more than friends." She sighed. "But you… made that…impossible. You kept me at arm's length. All I could think was that you were watching me bumbling around the pueblo when I didn't belong here."

"No! Of course you belong here. I was afraid with your fancy Los Angeles background, you wouldn't want a guy who came from the gutter," he answered in a thick voice. "I was doing it because I thought you would reject me, if you want to know the truth."

"Oh, Lord. Luke, you were so wrong." She raised her

head. "Then…then we were both so worried about Joe. He brought us together."

"He always wanted us to be together."

"I know. And I couldn't figure out how to make you have an honest conversation with me about anything important." She sprang across the room, her arms open. He caught her in his embrace and gathered her to him. "Luke, I love you," she murmured. "Last night with you was so wonderful. Then in the morning…I thought you had second thoughts about making love with me."

"I thought you'd be sorry you'd gone that far with me."

She made a snorting sound. "I was hoping it would be the beginning of something…not the end."

"The beginning," he said, as though he still couldn't believe that he was holding her in his arms and that they were having this discussion.

Looking like a man caught in a dream, he lowered his head, covering her lips with his. And she kissed him with all the emotion that welled inside her.

When he lifted his mouth and looked down into her face, his eyes were shining.

"This is no dream," she whispered. "It's real."

"Yes."

She turned and looked down the hall toward the bedrooms. "So are we done talking right now?"

He followed her gaze. "Oh yeah, *chiquita*," he agreed, taking her hand and walking with her down the hall.

"I used to hate it when you called me that."

"I know."

"Now…"

"Now, every time you hear it, you know I'm saying 'I love you.'"

TOM
ANN VOSS PETERSON

Chapter One

A flash of brown-gray fur stirred the shadows near the ruins of Sena Pueblo's ancient wall. Yellow eyes glowed from the darkness.

Cold sweat trickled between Roberto Sanchez's shoulder blades. He backed away from the window until he found himself pressed up against the bars of the tribal police station's holding cell. He was trapped. He had no way out.

The old stories whispered in his memory—stories of witches transforming themselves into animals to bring suffering and death. As a child, he used to huddle in his bed when the coyote calls echoed through the mountains. He'd imagine a coyote's shadow looming on the ceiling above him, a witch waiting to steal his heart, his soul.

Now, because of what he'd done, the coyote was outside. Waiting. Watching. And the bars designed to imprison him could never keep him safe.

He needed help. He needed protection.

Turning his back to the window, Roberto gripped the steel bars with shaking hands. "Gonzales?"

Silence.

Roberto gritted his teeth. Gonzales hated him. He'd made that clear when Roberto had tried to date his sister. But still, Gonzales was a tribal cop. It was his job to protect his people. Even the ones behind bars. "Gonzales? Are you here?"

Shuffling steps echoed from the adjoining office. An old woman peered at Roberto from the doorway, her head covered by a woven shawl. Shadows cloaked her eyes and settled into the worn creases of her skin. "Fred Gonzales is outside. I'm here to help you if I can."

Help him? Who was this woman? What was she talking about? Had she seen the coyote in the shadows? Roberto clung to the bars. This old woman could never protect him from a witch. Not unless she was practiced in witchcraft herself—a possibility he didn't even want to think about.

The lawyer.

Roberto looked down at the phone number scrawled on his hand. When Luke Cordova had turned him over to the tribal police, he'd given Roberto a number for a lawyer. A lawyer famous throughout the Santa Fe area for protecting the innocent and the weak.

Roberto only hoped Tom Lahi could protect him now. "You could help me by handing me a telephone. I want to call my lawyer."

TOM'S CELL PHONE RANG, its shrill sound echoing down the office building's dark hall. Maybe it was Paxton Gardner. The fat-cat art collector had asked Tom to meet him tonight to write a contract commissioning art from a local artist. But Gardner hadn't shown. Tom had not been happy to find he'd driven all the way to Santa Fe only to be stood up.

He pulled his phone off his belt and checked the readout. The number for the Sena Pueblo tribal police station glowed on the screen. A shot of adrenaline slammed into his bloodstream. Legal work for people like Gardner was necessary to pay the bills, but Tom took it on only to finance his true purpose: protecting his people. The people of Sena Pueblo. People such as whoever was at the other end of this phone line.

Tom hit the talk button. "Tom Lahi."

"The coyote is watching me. He's coming for me." The voice on the line was ragged, breathless.

"Who is this?"

"Sanchez."

Tom had heard that Luke Cordova and Ashley Donaldson had tracked down the man who'd murdered Luke's uncle Joe. "*Roberto* Sanchez?"

"Luke Cordova gave me your number. He said I should call you."

Tom frowned. It didn't make sense. If Roberto Sanchez murdered Joe, why would Luke give the man his number? "*Luke Cordova* referred you to me?"

"I didn't do it. I didn't kill Joe." Even though the phone connection crackled, there was something in the man's voice that rang loud and clear—desperation, sincerity, fear—Tom didn't know. But he had the feeling Roberto Sanchez was telling the truth.

Maybe Luke had gotten that same feeling. Maybe he had worried that Roberto was being railroaded for a crime he hadn't committed. Just as Luke had been railroaded years before. "Go on, Roberto."

"You have to help me. He's a witch. He doesn't want me to tell." Static fuzzed over the line.

"Hold on, let me try to get a better signal." Tom turned away from the entrance to Gardner's office suite and strode down the hall to the door. He pushed it open and stepped outside into the night. The signal improved, at least a little. "Now, slow down and explain."

"You have to help me. Please. He's outside the police station. He's coming for me."

"Who?"

"The coyote. He paid me to go into the desert and to get the gun. He told me where to find it."

Tom had never put a lot of stock in the beliefs of his people. Witchcraft and shape-shifting into animals made good stories to tell children and tourists, but that was the end of their significance. In Tom's experience, a federal justice system run by rich, white men was more threatening than any coyote or owl or snake. And humankind's greed and thirst for power did a better job of conjuring up evil than witchcraft ever could. "The coyote told you where to find the gun?"

"Yes."

"Who is this witch, Roberto?"

"I can't tell you over the phone. He's watching. He's listening. He'll cause me to die before his name crosses my lips. You have to come. You have to help me."

Tom started down the sidewalk in the direction of his truck. He didn't believe in witches and shape-shifting, but he did believe in protecting his people. And right now, Roberto needed protection—from a physical threat or nothing more than his own fear, Tom couldn't say. "I'll be right there, Roberto. Hold on."

TOM'S OLD PICKUP rattled and jolted over ruts in the dirt road leading to Sena Pueblo. The night was black but for the pinpoint light of stars. The moon had not yet risen over the mountains. Red dust swirled in the headlight beams.

Tom pushed his foot to the accelerator, punishing the shocks on his truck. The drive from Santa Fe to Sena Pueblo seemed to be taking twice as long as it normally did, even though he knew he was making good time.

Still, every moment must seem like an hour for a man in Roberto's situation. Tom needed to see the frightened man, to make sure he wasn't in real danger.

The holding cell and tiny police station was housed in a relatively modern adobe-style building on the pueblo's edge. The first thing he saw when he pulled in was Tribal Officer Fred Gonzales's frowning lips clenched around a hand-rolled cigarette stub.

Tom parked the truck and got out.

"What the hell do you want, Lahi?" Gonzales stuck out his barrel chest. Smoke puffed through his lips and into the air.

"I'm here to see my client."

"Sanchez? That piece of garbage is your client? You must be desperate for a fee." Gonzales tossed the butt to the dirt and ground it out with his heel. He stuck another cigarette between his lips. "Not that you're likely to get paid from a deadbeat janitor."

Tom kept his face a careful blank. Most of the tribal officers here and in the surrounding pueblos were honest men who wanted to help their people. Gonzales was nothing more than a bully with a uniform. Still, Tom had finally learned after a rough youth to only pick fights that mattered. And in murder cases on pueblo land, jurisdiction rested with the federal government, not Fred Gonzales. "So Roberto is inside."

Gonzales thrust out his barrel chest. "Until the FBI gets here. Now that I've done their job for them, all they have to do is pick him up."

As if on cue, the roar of an engine split the night. Tom turned toward the sound. The headlights from a sports utility vehicle bounced along the dirt road leading to the police station. The driver pulled in behind his truck and killed the engine. The FBI seal on the SUV's door glowed through darkness and swirling dust.

"The fibbies are early. A first. Must be someone new," Gonzales said, the cigarette wagging with each word. He flicked a lighter, the flame illuminating his permanent scowl. "Looks like old Roberto won't be here long."

"Long enough for me to talk to him." Tom strode for the station door.

"Would you look at that? Another first," Gonzales barked. "Hey, sweetheart."

Tom kept walking. He didn't have time for Gonzales's games or for suffering through an introduction to a new special agent. Still, he couldn't prevent himself from glancing over his shoulder.

The slip of a blonde slammed the door of the FBI vehicle and shot Gonzales a challenging glare. She looked as though she was masquerading as a boy with her hair cropped tight to the sides of her head in some sort of pixie hairstyle and her body hidden in a no-nonsense pantsuit. But no hairstyle could disguise those delicate features and no clothing could hide that purely feminine body. If anything, the contrast made her look more feminine than if she had been wearing a dress.

A strange feeling niggled at the back of his neck. As if he'd met this woman before. Another time. Another place. Hell, maybe another life. He turned away and finished his trek to the door.

"Tom?"

He stopped, hand in midreach, and turned around.

The pixie breezed past Gonzales, ignoring the tribal cop's lecherous leer, and marched straight for Tom. "Are you representing Roberto Sanchez?" She spoke in tones as short and businesslike as her haircut. But just as her boyish clothing and hair highlighted her femininity, her abrupt manner of speaking made her voice seem even more rich and womanly. The kind of voice made to whisper dirty words in the dark of night.

"That's right." He knew this woman. He knew her.

She stepped closer to the station entrance. The light fully illuminated her pixie face, her cute little turned-up nose, her big blue eyes.

Sure enough. "Jessie Gardner?"

A smile curved her lips and she was that girl again, the girl who'd followed him around like a starstruck fan back in the days he'd worked at Sandoval Fresh Foods, the days before Luke's arrest had changed his life for good.

He answered her sweet smile with a grin of his own. Her attentions back in those days had made him feel important, as though he mattered more than a nineteen-year-old pueblo boy with a bad job had a right to matter. Thinking of it, thinking of *her*, he couldn't help but smile. "You're with the FBI? I can't believe it."

The smile dropped from her lips and wariness shuttered her eyes. "I'm here to take the prisoner into federal custody. Where is he?"

Tom shook himself out of his reverie of the past. He had a job to do, too. "Inside. I was about to confer with him." He pushed the door open and stepped into the station, leaving Jessie Gardner waiting in the doorway.

He spotted Roberto in the single holding cell right away. But unlike most prisoners relieved to see their lawyer arrive, the janitor didn't race to the cell door. Instead he stood unmoving, back near the window, in the shadows.

"Roberto?" Tom stepped closer, willing his eyes to adjust, his mind to absorb the image in front of him. Roberto wasn't standing at all. He dangled a few inches off the floor, a leather belt suspending him from the neck.

Chapter Two

When Jessie finally stepped out of the tribal police station after securing the scene, the fresh night air hit her like a splash of cool water on a hot day. She breathed deeply, trying to rinse the stench of death's release from her nostrils. Her first case out of the Albuquerque office was supposed to have been simple—collect the prisoner at Sena Pueblo and take him into federal custody. Simple. Right. She'd known she was in trouble the moment she'd driven up to the pueblo police station and seen Tom Lahi. And if that hadn't been enough to send her knees shaking, now the prisoner she was supposed to have taken into custody was dead.

She rubbed her eyes with thumb and forefinger, trying to erase the image of the prisoner hanging by the belt around his neck, the pressure making his bloodshot eyes bulge, his face swollen and purple. There was nothing she could do for him now. Nothing except to find out what had happened to him. What had caused the kind of desperation that had led to his suicide. Or, if it wasn't a suicide, who had killed him. Either way, she had to treat his death as a homicide. At least until the evidence at the scene and the autopsy proved otherwise. And that included questioning the last people Sanchez had had contact with before he'd died.

In the parking area outside the station, Gonzales leaned into the open window of his SUV, talking on the radio and sucking on a cigarette as if nicotine were more precious to him than oxygen. He slipped the radio mike back into his vehicle as she approached. "The Feds are on their way."

"With a crime scene unit?"

"Yeah."

She nodded. "Were you here all night, Officer Gonzales?"

"Only time I left was to have a smoke. He must have waited until I stepped out to string himself up. Son of a bitch."

She eyed the glowing ash on the end of the cigarette. "You smoke a lot?"

"It's an addiction."

Obviously. "Was anyone else here?"

"No."

"Not all evening?"

"Not until Lahi showed up. And you." He squinted his eyes into slits. "You're not thinking of pinning the blame for this on me, are you?"

"I'm trying to get a better idea of what happened."

"I figured as much." He pulled the cigarette from his lips long enough to clear his throat and spit in the dirt. "I know women like you. Always trying to prove yourself. Stepping on the bodies of hardworking men on your way up the ladder. Can't just do your goddamn job."

Jessie's face grew hot. She'd had to prove herself to men like Gonzales since she'd decided to go into law enforcement. No, longer than that. Since she was born, starting with her father. And no matter what she did, it was never good enough. "Finding out what happened to the prisoner is my job."

"But blaming his suicide on me isn't."

"I'm not blaming anyone. I'm gathering facts. And one fact happens to be that the man was in your custody, Officer."

"And he killed himself to avoid being taken into federal custody. In my book, that lands on your shoulders, *special agent.*"

She took a breath of clean air and let the breeze fan her cheeks. She wasn't getting anywhere with Gonzales. The man was too busy covering his own ass to give her the answers she needed. Or maybe he really didn't have any answers. Maybe he was just incompetent.

She glanced around the parking lot for a moment before she spotted Tom. He paced in front of a small field of cornstalks still standing like broken skeletons from last fall's harvest. The breeze rattled the corn's brittle leaves. His boots scraped across dirt and stone.

Even after all these years, awareness of him shimmered over her skin, raising goose bumps. But unlike those days at the grocery where Tom had worked, she was no longer an insecure rich girl hoping to catch the handsome and older bad boy's attention. Now she was an FBI agent in search of answers. She pulled herself up and crossed the road.

He didn't look at her, not at first, though she could sense he knew she was there. His expression was hard, intense. Bronzed skin stretched taut over his high cheekbones. Lines dug into his forehead. She'd always thought he looked like a warrior as a young man, with his long black hair and the way his body moved with a sort of fierce agility. But even though he'd traded his long hair for a short businesslike crop, the fierceness was still there. And try as she might, she couldn't shake the warrior image. The only difference, she supposed, was that his battlefield was now the courtroom.

He stopped his pacing and turned his brown eyes on her. Eyes she'd never forgotten. But now instead of being filled with the rebellion of a rough youth, they ached with tragedy.

"I need to ask you some questions."

He nodded and took a deep breath. "Roberto called me tonight."

"To represent him?"

"To protect him. He was afraid."

She thought of Gonzales's charge. "Afraid to be taken into federal custody? To face justice?"

"No. He said he was innocent. Other than that, he hardly mentioned the case. Or federal custody."

"Then what was he afraid of?"

"The coyote outside his window."

She'd heard stories of shape-shifters. The Sena Pueblo people believed coyotes were often possessed by Native American witches as a vehicle to do harm. And though her father had scoffed at her naiveté more than once, a part of her had always believed the stories could be true. "He thought a witch was watching him?"

Tom narrowed his eyes as if trying to read her. "He said a witch wanted to keep him from telling what he knew about Joe Cordova's murder."

"What did he know?"

"He said he'd explain when I arrived." He grimaced, as if mentally berating himself for being too late to protect his client.

"Do you think his fear drove him to take his own life?"

"Not a chance. He didn't want to die. He was afraid

to die. So why would he take his own life? It doesn't make sense."

She had to admit it didn't. "But he was locked in a jail cell. Who could have reached him? Officer Gonzales said no one else was here tonight. No one but him."

Tom watched her out of the corner of his eye, his profile stark and angular against the distant glow of the snow-capped Sangre de Cristo Mountains. "That's what he said."

His meaning was as clear as the night air. "You think *Gonzales* might have had something to do with it?" She glanced in the direction of the glowing cigarette.

"It makes more sense than believing in witches, don't you think?"

"I'm not so sure."

A smile tilted one side of his mouth. "Your mind is still as open to pueblo culture as when you were a girl?"

A shiver rippled through her at the intimacy in his deep voice. "I try."

"You try harder than I do if you believe in witches."

They'd had this conversation more than once when she'd followed him around as he'd worked in the store. Tom loved his people, loved his heritage, but he didn't believe in the old stories, the power of the rituals, the possibility of magic, good or evil. In contrast, Jessie had always looked for something to believe in. At least until she'd grown up and realized that if she wanted respect, she'd better start believing in herself. "I must admit Gonzales isn't my favorite person on earth, but murder? Why would he do it?"

The smile fell from Tom's face and his expression became hard once again. "A few months ago Gonzales beat the hell out of Roberto at the Sena Casino. Word has it Gonzales promised to kill him the next time he looked at his sister."

"And you think Roberto sneaked a peek?"

Tom shrugged.

She bit her lower lip and considered the possibility. "If that's the case, this has nothing to do with Joe Cordova's murder."

"Or maybe Gonzales is crooked in many different ways."

"Do you have evidence of any of this?"

"As far as Roberto's death goes, Gonzales had opportunity. He had means. Enough for the U.S. Attorney to prove his prima facie case. If you could find a witness to the death threat, you'd even have motive."

Jessie frowned. Maybe it was the fact that Fred Gonzales was a fellow law enforcement officer…but it didn't feel right. "Why would he kill a man who's in custody in a jail where he's the only one with access? He places the suspicion smack on his own shoulders."

"What's the alternative? That a witch infiltrated the jail? That he took on the shape of a snake and slithered in?" Tom stared at the distant hulking shapes of the mountains, shaking his head. "I may be a pueblo man, but I'm more inclined to believe a real flesh-and-blood human was responsible for killing Roberto. Not magic."

Maybe or maybe not. But that wasn't the only alternative. "Then we're back to suicide."

A muscle along his jaw tightened. "I don't think it's suicide. But if it is, it's my fault."

"Your fault?"

"He said the witch was outside watching him. I promised I'd help him. Protect him. I didn't get here in time."

So that's why Tom couldn't face the possibility of suicide. Fear that he'd failed. She could understand that. Deep in the pit of her stomach, she fought the fear of failure every day.

Without thinking, she reached out and placed a hand on his arm. His flesh was firm and muscular under the crisp cotton of his white, button-down shirt. And so warm in the chill night.

When she had watched Tom stocking shelves all those years ago, he'd seemed like a god to her with his bronzed skin, powerful physique and knowledge of a mysterious and ancient culture she could never truly be part of no matter how much she wanted to believe. Tom had never seemed like flesh and blood. He had not seemed subjected to pain and emotion and frailty like the rest of the human race. But seeing his pain now, touching his warmth, he seemed to be stronger, to loom larger than he ever did at nineteen.

His biceps balled and hardened under her fingers. He watched her, his eyes clear and sharp and penetrating.

An emptiness hollowed her stomach and expanded into her chest. She couldn't do this. Couldn't look into his eyes. Couldn't touch him. Couldn't let herself think of how he'd affected her as a kid, how he affected her now. She had a job to do. An important job. And she couldn't fail.

Tom watched Jessie walk away. His arm felt cold where her hand had warmed it. The air felt empty where her presence and gentle scent had filled it.

He shook his head. He couldn't get over how the girl who'd followed him around Sandoval Fine Foods had grown into such a beautiful woman. And an FBI agent. He never would have guessed that. She'd always seemed so kind and sensitive as a girl. A beam of sweet sunshine back during those hard times.

Even now, hearing her voice, feeling her touch, had stirred warm feelings in him. She spoke to him in a woman's voice, touched him with the heat of a woman's touch. And he'd responded.

He rubbed a hand over his face. He might be attracted to Jessie—hell, that was only natural—but he couldn't afford to stand around thinking about her. After what had happened to Roberto tonight he didn't have time to entertain old daydreams. Not while Roberto's killer was roaming free.

Blocking the ache that settled into his bones, he spun on a heel and started walking back to his truck. He'd have to break the news to Roberto's mother. She should hear it from one of her own people—one who understood too well how tragedy could rip a family apart. And after he delivered the horrible news, he'd do whatever he could to bring her justice.

Chapter Three

Fresh from her morning shower, Jessie had just buttoned her blouse and downed a cup of coffee when a knock sounded on her hotel room door.

Tom Lahi?

Her heart paused for a second before resuming its beat. The thought didn't make sense. Tom wouldn't come all the way down to Santa Fe from the pueblo, would he? And he certainly wouldn't show up at her hotel, no matter how intent he was on learning what had happened to his client the night before.

Besides, seeing him was the last thing she needed. Last night she'd felt as trembly around him as she had when she was an awkward, vulnerable teen. If she wanted to prove herself in the FBI, she had to be twice as strong and capable as a male agent. She sure as hell couldn't afford trembly.

Peering through the peephole, she stared into her father's ice-blue eyes. "Dad?" She unlocked the door and pulled it open.

Paxton Gardner studied her under furrowed gray eyebrows. "What's this about a death up at Sena Pueblo last night? Why didn't you call me?"

Jessie gripped the door so hard her fingers ached.

She should be used to her father's demands, his disapproval when she inevitably failed him, but she wasn't. It cut her fresh every time. "So you heard about Roberto Sanchez."

"Of course I heard. What I can't figure out is why I didn't hear it from you."

"You know I can't talk about an investigation." She swung the door wide and stood to the side, leaving an open swath where her father could enter.

He didn't move. "I never wanted to have a daughter in law enforcement. But I'm living with it. I even called in favors to get you assigned to this area. The least you could do is tell me what's going on."

The fresh stab of pain dulled and scabbed over with anger as it always did under one of his assaults. "I wanted to think you pulled strings to get me assigned to the Albuquerque field office because you wanted me near you and Mom. I should have known your motives weren't that warm and fuzzy."

"These people are important to me, Jessica."

"'These people?' The victim wasn't one of the artists you buy and sell. You have nothing to worry about."

"Was it suicide?"

"You're not listening. I can't talk about it with you." She grabbed her suit jacket and stuffed her arms into the sleeves. "I have to go."

"Where?"

She let out a frustrated breath. She might as well tell him. Save him the trouble of following her. "Roberto Sanchez's autopsy."

He didn't move from the doorway, his wide shoulders blocking her way. "I'll be waiting for your phone call to tell me the findings."

"I'll fill you in once the case is closed." She dodged

around him, leaving her father standing alone in the mouth of her hotel room, the door agape.

JESSIE SLAMMED THE DOOR of her SUV and strode toward the lone trailer, in the middle of the desert, that Fred Gonzales called home. Her feet ached from spending the morning witnessing Roberto Sanchez's autopsy and the rest of the day tracking down details of Gonzales's depressing life. A sister who hated him for chasing off every potential boyfriend she'd ever had; an ex-wife all too eager to string him up for murder, guilty or not; two kids who didn't seem to know who he was. It had been one long, drawn-out bummer of a day, not to mention the uplifting visit from her father this morning.

She inhaled a deep breath of cool evening air and surveyed the area. The sun had already sunk behind the horizon, turning the snowcapped peaks of the Sangre de Cristos as bloodred as their name described. At least she could understand one thing about Gonzales—why he chose to live out here. The setting was truly soul-filling. Magic.

The sound of stone scraping stone caught her attention. She spun around. Nothing but low, scrubby juniper dotted the desert floor behind her, quickly falling into shadow.

She raked a hand through her cropped hair. She was tired. She was depressed. Now she was hearing things. She turned back to Gonzales's trailer and resumed walking, her boots crunching dirt and stone. There it was again. Another set of steps adding to the sound of her own. An animal? A human? She stopped again, whirled around.

Nothing.

She really was losing it. Either that or the pueblo legends of witchcraft had more reality to them than Tom believed. Unlike him, deep down she'd always felt that magic existed in the world. Good and bad. But that possibility wasn't reassuring at the moment. She'd rather face a flesh-and-blood foe, one she knew how to handle, than tangle with the supernatural.

She took another deep breath and turned back toward Gonzales's trailer. But this time she reached under her suit jacket and unsnapped the flap of her shoulder holster. Just in case.

She'd almost reached the trailer when movement flashed behind her. She reached for her pistol and pulled it from her holster.

An arm snaked around her throat. Another came down hard on her wrist.

Pain shot up her forearm. Her fingers went slack. Her weapon fell to the ground, clattering against stone. "Stop. I'm FB—"

The arm tightened, cutting off her voice, cutting off her air.

She grabbed the arm, digging her fingers into human flesh. She kicked back, connecting with a shin.

A man's voice spit out a curse.

She kicked again, driving the solid heel of her boot into his leg at the tender part of the knee.

The grip on her throat loosened.

She gasped a breath into burning lungs. Lowering her chin, she opened her mouth and sank her teeth into the man's arm.

More curses. The hard body jolted backward and released her, pushing her forward.

She reached out to catch herself, her hands hitting rock. Pain shuddered up her arms.

A knee drilled into her back, forcing her flat. A hand

clasped the back of her head and pushed her face into the red dirt.

She gasped, trying to breathe, but inhaled only dust. Coughs racked her body.

"We don't want Feds around here," a voice snarled, deep and guttural.

She tried to answer, to tell him to go to hell, but all she could do was choke.

The knee drove harder into her back.

A lump on the ground beneath her dug into her hip. Her gun. She moved her hand slowly toward it, inch by inch, praying he wouldn't notice in the dusk.

"We have our own ways of justice around here. The way we've always handled things. We don't need you to butt in."

Her fingers touched the Glock's grip. So far, so good. He was apparently so intent on delivering his message, he didn't feel her move beneath him. But she still couldn't get the weapon out from under her body. Not without him feeling her lift off the ground, not without the movement giving her away.

She sucked in a breath, taking in more dust than air. She erupted into a coughing fit. That was it. She forced herself to cough harder, bucking her body upward ever so slightly as she retched and gasped.

She pulled the gun out from under her and flipped her body over, tossing the man off balance. She whipped the Glock in front of her in firing position. Ready to shoot.

But no one was there.

What the hell? Scrambling to her feet, she scraped the landscape with her gaze. Shadows of juniper stretched long in the twilight. The cool air seemed to echo with stillness. It was as if no one had ever been here. As if the arm around her throat, the knee in her back, the voice—all of it—had been her imagination.

Or magic.

She shook her head. The man was real. Flesh and blood. She'd kicked his shin. She'd bit his arm. She turned in a full circle, squinting at every plant, every rock, every shadow. Nothing. She was alone.

But she didn't feel alone.

Using the juniper for cover, she crept toward her SUV. She needed help. Backup. The Sena Pueblo tribal police station wasn't far, maybe eight miles. An officer shouldn't take long to reach her.

She made it to her vehicle and reached for the door latch.

A rifle shot cracked the still air. The driver's window in front of her shattered.

Jessie flattened herself to the ground.

Another shot reverberated off rock and stone. The tire closest to her head whooshed air.

So much for magic. She had to find cover and she had to do it now.

She crawled along the desert floor on her belly. Rock bit into her knees. Beaver tail cactus stabbed her hands. She circled the SUV. Once behind the vehicle, she raised herself to a crouch and returned fire. If she could keep the vehicle between herself and the shooter, she might be able to hold him off long enough for backup to arrive. But first she had to reach dispatch.

She ducked low, pulled her cell phone from her belt and flipped it open. Lights flashed across the small screen as the phone tried to lock on to a signal. Seconds lengthened to a minute. Nothing.

Damn. She would have to use the radio in the truck. She squeezed off a few more rounds to keep the ri-

fleman in place and opened the passenger door. The
dome light came on. She reached for the switch and
plunged the vehicle's interior into darkness.

A rifle shot echoed against the mountains. The windshield shattered. Glass peppered Jessie. She stretched
across the seat. Snagging the wire with her fingertips,
she dragged the radio toward her.

The truck listed as a bullet shredded a second tire.

Pressing the talk button, she called for the dispatcher.
Static answered her. She tried again. Nothing. It was as
if something was blocking the signal.

She forced herself to inhale, scooping breath after
breath into hungry lungs. Who the hell was shooting at
her? Gonzales? Whoever it was, she didn't know how
long she could hold off a sharpshooter with a rifle when
all she had was a handgun. He was probably on the
move right now, circling to get a clear shot.

She hunkered down behind the SUV and eyed Gonzales's trailer. Whether Gonzales was the shooter or
not, his trailer appeared to be vacant. Once darkness fell,
maybe she could cross to the trailer. Maybe he had a
phone inside. Maybe…

Behind her, the roar of an engine cut the stillness.
Headlights wound along the dirt road toward her.

Her heart rattled against her rib cage. Chambering a
round, she leveled her weapon on the pickup.

The driver slid into a U-turn and stopped next to her,
kicking a cloud of dust into the air. He threw the passenger door open just as gunfire exploded around them.

Jessie looked into the dark eyes of Tom Lahi.

"Get in," he yelled over the engine and the bullets
pinging off the SUV. "And you might want to hurry."

Chapter Four

As soon as Jessie dove into the passenger seat, Tom stomped on the accelerator. Dust churned into the air, tires grabbing for purchase. The truck raced down the dirt road. Away from the gunman. Away from the bullets.

Each bump and pothole jolted through him and threatened to tear the wheel from his hands. He didn't slow down. He didn't even take a breath until they reached the paved highway. "What the hell happened?"

"I was ambushed." She looked pale in the dashboard's glow, as ethereal as a ghost, as fragile as crystal. Red dust covered her face and clothes, as if she'd just escaped the fires of hell.

He focused on the highway. "Did you see who it was?"

"No." She blew out a frustrated breath. "But I can guess. Though I did miss seeing his cigarette glowing in the night."

"That wasn't Gonzales shooting at you."

"How do you know?"

"My friend Rico's art gallery was broken into tonight. Gonzales was in Santa Fe working with the cops. I just saw him before I drove up here."

"So if that wasn't Gonzales, who was it?"

"Someone who doesn't want you to find out who

killed Roberto. Or Joe Cordova." He glanced at her out of the corner of his eye. "The only thing taken in the gallery theft were six paintings by Joe Cordova."

"You think the burglary is related to his murder?"

He shrugged. "I thought you should know about it."

"Thanks. I'll check it out. I reviewed the evidence against Roberto today."

"And?"

"It's thin."

Tom nodded. He had known in his gut it was a setup. A phone call to Luke had confirmed he shared Tom's doubts. "And Roberto's death? Did I convince you last night that he was murdered?"

"The autopsy convinced me today."

"It showed he was murdered? How?"

She considered for a moment, as if deciding whether to share the details.

"Listen, I was his lawyer. And a little information is the least you can give me after I saved your life tonight." Just thinking about her out here alone with nothing but a little handgun for protection made him want to wrap her in his arms. A gesture he couldn't imagine she'd appreciate.

"How did you know I was out here?"

He tapped the police radio built into the dash of his pickup. One of his rare spending splurges. "I use it to keep track of what's going on around here. It helps to know when my people might need me."

"You heard my call? I got back nothing but static."

"It might not have reached dispatch, but it reached me on the highway. So, you see? You owe me the autopsy results."

The corners of her lips curved slightly upward and she let out a long sigh. "He has two belt marks on his neck. The angle of the first is straight across. He was strangled from behind before he was strung up."

Tom let the picture sink into his mind. Roberto, frightened, waiting anxiously for Tom's arrival, attacked by whoever it was who wanted to silence him. "I was right. Roberto didn't end his life because of fear. The person he feared stole his life from him." And he'd gotten there too late.

"That's what it looks like."

He veered onto the dirt road leading to Sena Pueblo, but he didn't swing into the police station.

"Where are you going? I have to report the shooting."

"No one's at the station."

"Everyone's down in Santa Fe?"

"There are only two tribal officers on duty. Gonzales will be tied up in Santa Fe for a long while yet. The other officer was called to a domestic. I heard the call on the radio and I know the family. He'll be lucky if he's back for breakfast."

"What about the shooter?"

"He's long gone by now. Do you know what that land is like around there? There's no way anyone could hope to catch up to him tonight. And the cops will have to wait until daylight to try to track him. Even then, I'm betting they won't be able to find much."

"I need my vehicle."

"The only towing service in the area with a flatbed truck isn't open until tomorrow morning." Tom slowed the truck to a crawl as he entered the rough, narrow road that wound around the pueblo's kiva, the Catholic church and the adobe houses with their tiny yards. A dog watched them from under an old truck, its eyes glowing yellow in the headlights.

"Where are you taking me?" Jessie asked.

"My place."

Her elegant eyebrows arched. "Excuse me?"

"I live close to the police station. We can check to see if Gonzales gets back in a few hours. Besides, I need to talk to you."

"About what?"

"I'll explain when we get inside."

Jessie tried to ignore the shiver slinking over her skin as she stepped past Tom and through the open door of his tidy adobe home. Just being near the man made her feel like that awkward teenager. Or like a damsel in distress, as evidenced by her need for rescue tonight. The last thing she wanted was to spend time with him alone, in the intimacy of his home. But he was Roberto's lawyer, and as far as she knew, the last person who'd talked to the poor man. If Tom knew anything that would help her case, she needed to hear it. She'd just have to push her old feelings about him out of her mind.

Jessie braced herself and walked down a hall that opened into a modest living room. A baseball game flickered on the small television.

Tom switched on a lamp, illuminating the beautiful assortment of Sena Pueblo paintings, pottery and rugs decorating the room. "Hey, Emilio."

A boy, no more than ten years old, blinked up at them from the sofa. "Hi." He eyed Jessie, a frown puckering his round face.

"This is Jessie. Jessie, Emilio."

She had no idea Tom had children. Was he married? Disappointment stabbed her at the possibility. Shoving the ridiculous feeling away, she smiled at the boy. He was adorable. "Hello, Emilio. What are you watching?"

The boy punched the remote. The television went dark and silent. "Just stupid stuff."

"Baseball isn't stupid." She picked up the remote and switched the set back on. "The Diamondbacks. Cool."

"It's just a preseason game."

"Listen, spring training is important. That's where you can check out all the pitchers and get a feel for the new free agents. Do you play?"

Emilio nodded. A smile touched his lips.

"I'll bet you're good."

His little face fell. "My dad says I suck. I'll never be good enough to play on a real team."

His tone was matter-of-fact, but his words hit Jessie with the force of a closed fist. She glared at Tom. How could he say such a thing? And to his own son? It sounded like something from her father's mouth.

Tom held up his hands in front of him as if protecting himself. "I'm not Emilio's dad, if that's what you're thinking."

"You're not?" She looked back to the little boy so at home in front of Tom's television. Questions bounced around her mind.

"Emilio likes to visit sometimes. I leave the door open for him. He and I are baseball buddies."

Judging from the way the boy ducked his head, Tom wasn't telling the whole story. But Jessie knew enough not to ask. "That's great. My dad didn't have much use for baseball either. You don't know how many times I wished I had a baseball buddy growing up."

The smile found its way back to Emilio's face. He glanced at a clock perched on the tiny fireplace mantel. "My mom's home now. Gotta go."

Concern knit Tom's brows. "You sure?"

Emilio nodded. "She'll worry."

Emilio gave Jessie one last smile and scampered out the door.

Jessie looked at Tom. "So what was that really about?"

"His home life isn't great. He comes here when he needs to."

An understatement, she was sure. A tight ache throbbed in her chest. Sadness for an innocent little boy. And admiration for the man who sheltered him. "That's a noble thing to do."

Tom brushed her comment aside with a wave of his hand. "Why don't you sit down? We can talk."

Jessie nodded. A good idea. She'd come face-to-face with enough of Tom Lahi's admirable qualities for one night. First he'd risked his life to save hers. And now watching him with little Emilio made it clear that the nineteen-year-old who had treated her so kindly when she was a smitten girl had grown up to be a caring, sensitive man. She'd better hear what he had to say and get back on the road before she lost her head and touched him again. She sat on the couch.

Tom lowered himself into a chair facing her. "You need my help."

His help? He didn't believe she could handle the case on her own? Doubt stabbed into her like a sharp blade into tender skin. She drew in a measured breath. "I can handle a murder investigation just fine. I don't need help."

"I shouldn't have put it that way. I'm sure you've worked many cases and done a great job. I'm just saying I can help with this particular case."

She eyed him. She knew she was being defensive. But the truth was, she was so used to people being skeptical of her abilities, and she'd worked so hard to prove herself.... "How can you help?"

"I know the culture. I know the Sena people. We don't like talking to strangers. Outsiders. And even though you grew up in Santa Fe, you're still an outsider."

As if she needed the reminder. She was an outsider in the society she'd grown up in just as much as she was in the pueblo. "What's in it for you?"

"I want to see justice done. Same as you."

She was sure he did, but that wasn't the answer she was looking for. "And you feel guilty for Roberto Sanchez's death."

"Guilty?" He shrugged, the movement uncharacteristically tense and rigid. "I suppose that could be true. I told Roberto I'd help him. I didn't."

"You tried."

"Trying isn't good enough."

"Sometimes trying is all you can do."

He leaned forward and gripped the arms of his chair. "It's not all I can do. I can help you find Roberto's murderer. And I can clear his name. I can at least give his family that much."

"Do you always feel this much responsibility for your clients?"

"Shouldn't I?"

"I suppose you should. It's just…rare." But then, a lot about Tom Lahi was rare. And despite her better judgment, she wanted to know more. "Why are you so dedicated to your work? To your people?"

Heaving a sigh, he leaned back in his chair. "When I was nineteen, my friend Luke Cordova was arrested for armed robbery."

"I remember." Tom had quit his job at the grocery store after Luke's arrest, and he'd disappeared from her life. She couldn't count the times she'd thought of him after that. Worried about him. Missed the way he'd talked to her. The way he'd listened to her as if what she thought mattered.

He nodded. "Then you also remember Luke was finally proven innocent."

"Yes." The thought of his friend spending five years behind bars was horrible. Both for Luke and for Tom. And it had obviously had a huge impact on his life. "That's why you feel the need to protect your people? Because you couldn't protect your friend when you were nineteen?"

"Watching Luke get railroaded and not being able to do anything to help nearly killed me. So when he went to prison, I decided to go to law school."

She nodded, an even more detailed picture of the adult Tom taking shape. One even more attractive. More compelling. "And that's why you live here?"

"I like it here."

She glanced around the room, taking in the gently curved walls and doorways, the artwork, the rugs. "I can see why. It's nice. Comfortable. But not many lawyers would choose to live in a tiny house in the pueblo."

"Not rich enough?"

"Not successful-looking."

"I don't measure success with money."

"No, you measure it by your ability to protect your people." She could hardly believe she was talking to him this way. She should keep her mouth shut. But she couldn't seem to stop. "That's why you still live in the pueblo. And that's why you have a police scanner in your truck. Roberto Sanchez's murder means you aren't successful. And Joe Cordova's, too, for that matter."

He swallowed, grimacing as if her words were bitter going down. "I just want justice. For Joe and Roberto. And for their families." He peered into her eyes, the look as piercing and intimate as a touch.

A flutter spread along her nerves.

"I didn't have much of a family growing up," Tom told her. "My dad died in an accident before I was four.

My mother had a hard time of it. My friends Luke and Rico were my only real family."

"And after Luke was convicted…"

"Rico moved away. He couldn't stand to be in the pueblo after that. He moved back to Santa Fe recently, but he won't return to the pueblo."

A tightness filled her throat. "You lost your family a second time."

He nodded. "And there wasn't a damn thing I could do about it. I've never been so helpless in my life."

"So you decided to become the champion instead of the victim."

"I guess so. That's why you have to let me work with you on this case. I can't just sit by and do nothing. I won't."

She knew better than to agree to working with Tom, to being near him day after day, to exposing herself to feelings, to vulnerabilities she wanted no part of. But something inside her wouldn't let her say no. Not when he needed this so badly. And not when something inside her wanted it, as well. "All right."

"We're a team?"

"Like you said, you know the culture. The people. And after tonight, it seems I need someone to watch my back."

Chapter Five

Tom climbed the steps leading from the public parking lot to the spot where Rico Tafoya's gallery perched on Santa Fe's Canyon Road. Jessie walked in front of him, her hips swaying with each step. Averting his eyes, he concentrated on the ground.

After he'd driven her back to her hotel room last night, he'd spent most of the night thinking of her. Picturing the sparkle of interest in her eyes when she'd talked baseball with Emilio. The snap of anger and sadness when she'd learned of the little boy's tragic family life. And the way she'd prodded Tom himself with questions in that low, intimate voice, and he'd felt himself open like a cactus flower in April.

All the things he'd told her about losing his friends—the only real family he'd known—he'd never told anyone else. But Jessie clearly wasn't like anyone he'd ever met. He'd sensed that even when she was a lonely teen following him around at the store. Jessie had a generous heart. A heart that could embrace the baseball aspirations of a ten-year-old boy as easily as pull the poison from a thirty-year-old man's tragic memories.

He shook his head and focused on the Milagro Gallery. He was getting ahead of himself, way ahead. Jessie and he were working together to solve a case, nothing more. The rest was merely his loneliness talking. They'd come to the gallery to find out if last night's burglary, in which only Joe's paintings had been stolen, had had anything to do with Joe's murder. Or Roberto's. That's what he needed to focus on. Helping Jessie. Winning justice for Joe and Roberto. Giving their families some sense of peace.

Reaching the top of the stairs, Tom walked beside Jessie. "Luke Cordova and Ashley Donaldson said they'd meet us at the gallery. I thought you might want to talk to them about Roberto's arrest. And about Joe."

"Excellent. I was hoping to see them this morning, but coordinating the search for the shooter took longer than I'd hoped." She glanced at him. The late-morning sun sparkled in her short, blond hair. "You were right about the police not being able to track down the man who attacked me at Gonzales's trailer. Even the dogs they brought in from Albuquerque this morning couldn't hold the trail once it disappeared into those gorges surrounding the mountains."

"Not surprising."

She shook her head. "Last night I could have sworn I heard someone behind me, but when I turned around, no one was there. And after he attacked me, when I escaped, he was suddenly gone, as well. And now even the tracking dogs couldn't hold his trail. The way he disappeared, I might be inclined to believe he was a witch." She tilted her head to eye him, as if waiting for his reaction.

Tom let an uneasy chuckle escape his lips. "A witch who transformed himself into an owl and flew away?"

"Coyotes and owls?"

"Sometimes snakes and other animals, too."

"I thought snakes were supposed to be good."

"It depends on the beliefs of the particular Pueblo. Sena Pueblo picked up the Spaniards' more Christian beliefs about snakes."

"That they're evil."

"That they're tools used by evil."

She nodded, as if she understood.

At least one of them did.

"Why don't you believe in the old stories?" she asked.

"Why? Maybe because the evil I've seen in the world has come from ordinary people doing cruel but ordinary things to each other."

"And the good?"

"I haven't seen much of that."

She let out a sigh.

He shook his head. The last thing he wanted was for her to be sighing over him. "The old stories and beliefs have never protected my people. They have never provided jobs. They haven't kept families together. They haven't ensured justice."

"Those are complicated issues, Tom."

"Exactly. Not things that can be fixed by a few rituals or stories about shape-shifting witches."

"Stories, rituals, beliefs may not provide easy answers, but they do provide hope. Don't you think? Strength? Things people need to search out the solutions to tough problems?"

The last thing either of them needed was to get into some sort of discussion about the power of religion when they should be tracking down the truth about a murder. He held up his hands, palms out. "Listen, I believe in justice. Fair treatment. Let's let it go at that." He glanced at the gallery door. "And what do you say we go in?"

She flashed him a conciliatory smile. "Right behind you."

He pushed the door open. As he followed her across the threshold, a mix of acoustic guitar and Native American flutes washed over him. The scent of piñon from a burning smudge stick hung in the air. Rico, Luke and Ashley stood near a sculpture of a horse, its alabaster lines curved and graceful. After the introductions, Luke and Ashley filled Jessie in on Joe's strange behavior before his death and the way they had caught Roberto with the gun that killed Joe.

Once she'd heard their stories, asked a number of questions and jotted a page of notes, Jessie turned to Rico. "I understand only six paintings were taken in the burglary last night. Isn't that odd? You have an abundance of artwork on display."

Rico nodded casually. But Tom could tell that under the deliberately easygoing facade, his friend had been shaken by the burglary. "Joe's paintings are worth a lot of money. But there are other pieces here that are worth more. Pieces the burglars didn't touch."

"Maybe they didn't know what the other pieces are worth."

"Not a chance. Whoever stole the paintings knew exactly what they were looking for."

"Why do you think that?"

"They only missed one Joe Cordova in the whole gallery, yet they were in and out of here within minutes. Someone who could pick out six Joe Cordova's that quickly would know what the rest of this stuff is worth, too."

Jessie nodded and made a note.

Two men appeared behind Rico. Tom recognized one as Rico's assistant, Jay Soto. Dressed in his usual chambray shirt, blue jeans and superior expression, Jay glared at Rico as if mentally tapping his foot with impatience.

Rico turned to his assistant. "What is it, Jay?"

"Raul has brought more of his pottery."

Rico eyed the other man, who Tom noticed looked even shorter, rounder and older than he was next to the tall, thin and young Jay. Rico's forehead furrowed in a frown. "I'm sorry, Raul. I have all the pottery I can display right now. I told you that."

Raul splayed worn palms, arguing his case. "This is the best work I've ever done. You must, at least, look."

Behind Raul, Jay rolled his eyes.

Rico turned to Jessie. "If you'll excuse me?"

Jessie nodded. "I'll call if I have any more questions."

Rico and the potter moved away, but Jay hovered, as if hoping to eavesdrop.

Jessie glanced at him, then shifted her focus to Ashley. "That's an interesting necklace you're wearing. So unusual."

Ashley touched the amulet at her throat with her fingertips. "It belonged to my birth mother."

"It's beautiful," Jessie said.

Light green turquoise set in a disk of silver, it truly was beautiful. And very different from any piece Tom had seen before.

Ashley smiled sadly. "Thank you. I'm sorry we can't be more help in finding Joe's killer. I still can't believe he's gone."

Jessie offered her hand to Ashley. "I'm so sorry for your loss. I appreciate the help. And if I need anything more, I'll contact you."

Tom watched Jay Soto meander away, apparently giving up on learning any juicy news. Good. The last thing they needed were details of Joe's and Roberto's deaths scattered around town as the newest gossip. After saying their goodbyes to Ashley and Luke, Tom and Jessie turned to leave.

"Excuse me," a low voice said from behind them.

Tom spotted Charlotte Reyna peering at them from behind a display of hand-worked deer hides.

Charlotte brushed her thick black hair from her face, her dark gaze intent on Jessie. "You're the FBI agent looking for Joe's killer, aren't you?"

"Yes," Jessie said. "And you are?"

"Charlotte Reyna. I want to show you something." Charlotte motioned them to follow her into the area screened from the rest of the gallery by the hides. She nodded to a painting tucked into the corner.

The distinctive colors and shapes of the desert scene made Tom's heart thump. "This is the Joe Cordova painting the thief missed."

Charlotte nodded.

Jessie angled her head, studying the painting. "What did you want to show me?"

"The area in this painting."

Tom narrowed his eyes. The area did look familiar. The severe cut of the narrow canyon. The boulders standing sentinel near the spring. The slash of orange rock along the cliff wall. "Is this in the northwest corner of Sena Pueblo land?"

"Yes. It's an area Joe depicts in many of his paintings."

"And?" he prodded.

"It holds the answers."

"To what?"

"To who killed Joe. And others."

Tom narrowed his eyes on Charlotte. "How do you know this?"

"I just do."

"If you have evidence concerning these murders, you

must turn it over to me, Charlotte," Jessie said in a steady voice.

Charlotte focused on Jessie. "I don't have any evidence. Joe always told me that a painting should tell a story. Joe painted two areas over and over again. Black Canyon where he was killed and this place. I think he was trying to tell a very important story. You have to go there."

Tom frowned at Charlotte. Though he hadn't seen much of her since they were all children together in the pueblo, he'd always thought of her as honest and straightforward. Her grandmother was a neighbor of his and a woman he respected. But he knew damn well Charlotte was keeping something from them now. He could feel it. Maybe the years she'd spent away from the pueblo studying art in upstate New York had changed her. "You have to do a better job of explaining than that, Charlotte."

"I can't."

"Jessie is not going to go chasing around through the desert based on what you've given us."

Jessie met Tom's gaze. "Actually, I am."

"What?"

"Will you take me there?"

"There's no road. The road ends at Black Canyon. It's a long hike from there across sacred pueblo land." And there would be no one to call for help. He tried to shut out last night's memories of the crack of rifle fire, bullets aimed at Jessie.

"Then I'll hike." She set her chin. "If you don't want to go with me, that's fine. Just show me how to get there on a map."

He let out a defeated breath. As if he'd ever consider that option. "All right. I'll take you. But we'll borrow my neighbor's horses and approach from another direction. It's a bit farther, but we can make better time on horseback." And if someone decided to take pot shots at them, they could escape in a hurry.

THE WITCH STEPPED BACK into the shadow of a juniper and watched Jessica Gardner and Tom Lahi walk down the steps to the parking lot. They had wandered into the gallery unfocused, but they had marched out with purpose. That could only mean one thing. They had learned something. Something that had put them on his trail.

Damn Joe Cordova. Damn him for being so weak. For turning his cowardice into guilt.

He should have taken care of Joe long ago. Instead he'd waited. And now he had to clean up the mess Joe had caused.

He'd started with Joe's paintings. He'd stolen six from the Milagro Gallery last night. But more were out there. In other galleries, perhaps. In private collectors' homes. He needed to find them.

Already he could feel that someone was seeing what he or she shouldn't see. Knowing what he or she shouldn't know. He could tell by the subtle shifting of energy. The distortion in his visions. Someone was inching closer to the truth.

Chapter Six

Tom swung a leg over his mare and dismounted. She was cool now after walking the last two miles to the orange cliff, so he dropped the reins, ground-tying her near the spring and giving her the opportunity to drink.

Jessie did the same with her gelding, though her dismount was a little stiff.

"Sore?"

"I haven't ridden this much since pony club when I was a kid."

He couldn't help but smile. Here his neighbor encouraged him to ride the horses he kept in his backyard whenever Tom wanted, and yet, he hadn't ridden in months. He'd forgotten how much he enjoyed riding. Of course, it may not have been the riding he missed as much as Jessie's company.

Forcing his mind off Jessie and onto the reason they'd ridden all this way, he gestured to the wide vein of orange rock in the cliff that caught the sunlight, bright as flame. "This is the spot."

Jessie squinted up at the rock. "Just like Joe's painting."

Tom pointed to the south, in the direction of Santa Fe. "Black Canyon, the spot where Joe was shot, is that way. He might have been coming here when he died."

"I've seen the photos and read the reports filled out by Sena Pueblo's tribal officers, but I'd like to look over that area myself, as well. Do you think we'll have time today?"

Tom squinted up at the sun. "We'd better get moving. We don't have many hours until dark, and we have a long ride back. Once we put up the horses, we can drive to Black Canyon."

They walked toward the cliff, searching among rock and juniper and the occasional beavertail cactus for any clue to why this area was so important to Joe Cordova. And why Charlotte had insisted they come here. The sun beat down on them as minutes added up to hours. Sweat beaded on Tom's brow and dripped into his eyes. Just when he was about to curse Charlotte Reyna's infernal goose chase and call it a day, he spotted something white protruding from the *bajada,* the fan-shaped pile of earth at the foot of the cliff eroded from the cliff's wall and deposited by rain water. At one point, when the arroyo had gushed with water, it had cut into the sediment and swept part of the cliff downstream. Sun-bleached branches of juniper stuck out into the dry streambed.

No. Not juniper.

"Jessie." He pointed to the spot and strode toward it.

Jessie followed him. Reaching the spot, he looked down into the empty eye sockets of a human skull. His heartbeat thundered in his ears, drowning out the wind whistling in the cliff above.

Jessie stepped beside him. "My God, Tom. Bones. Human bones. A whole skeleton." She dropped to her knees, scrambling in her bag for her camera. Pulling it out, she began snapping pictures.

Tom knelt beside her and pointed to a dull gleam near the skull. "And look at this."

She leaned closer. A fine chain circled the neck of the

skeleton and attached to a piece of jewelry partially buried in gravel and silt. The pawn's silver-and-turquoise gleam caught a ray of sunlight. "It's a necklace of some kind."

Jessie captured a few more pictures from different angles. Once she'd documented the position of the necklace around the skeleton's neck, she caught the chain and gently pulled the stone where they could examine it. Light green turquoise stones set in heavy tooled silver. A necklace identical to the one they'd seen this morning. "It's the same as the amulet Ashley Donaldson was wearing."

"She said the one she was wearing was her birth mother's. That her father gave it to her mother before he disappeared." A bad feeling slammed into Tom's gut, as if he'd been punched. He let out a breath. "Damn. I hope there's not some kind of connection. Poor Ashley has been through enough."

Jessie opened her mouth to answer just as an inhuman shriek rent the air.

The horses. Tom sprang to his feet and raced down the arroyo toward the spring. Jessie scrambled after him.

A few feet from the water, the horses danced and threw their heads. The gelding reared in the air and shrieked again.

Tom slowed his pace and held out a calming hand to the horse. "Easy. Whoa, boy."

The animal blew through flared nostrils and flashed the whites of his eyes.

Tom searched the desert floor for what had the horse so spooked. He heard the high-pitched rattle before he saw its source. A sound like a mother shushing her child. He froze in his tracks.

Jessie panted up alongside. "What's wrong with them?"

Tom pointed in front of the gelding. There it was, curled in attack pose. "A rattler."

"My God. Aren't rattlers supposed to be dormant this time of year?" She unsnapped her shoulder holster.

The sound grew louder. The snake turned its attention to them.

Apparently seeing their chance, the horses bolted. They raced out of the canyon and down the arroyo, shod hooves sparking against stone, loose reins flying behind them.

"No." Jessie lunged forward as if to race after them. Tom grabbed her arm.

"We can't let them get away."

"In front of you. Look."

She glanced down. And gasped. The snake had slithered to within a few feet of her. It curled, rattle poised in the air.

"Back up slowly." Tom pulled her backward. One step. Two steps. "Shoot it."

Pulling the Glock from her shoulder holster, Jessie leveled the barrel on the snake's head. She squeezed off a shot.

The serpent moved sharply to the side and disappeared into a silvery clump of rabbit brush.

What the hell?

Suddenly a hiss erupted from behind them.

Tom and Jessie whipped around as one.

The snake lunged just as Tom pulled her out of the way.

Jessie regained her balance and took another shot. But this time, as she pulled the trigger, the snake seemed to vanish into thin air.

Tom stared at the spot where it had disappeared, expecting it to leap out at them at any moment. His pulse pounded in his ears as if marking the seconds as they ticked by. Where had the thing gone?

Finally, Jessie lowered her weapon and glanced at Tom. "What happened?"

Unease grasped the back of his neck like a cold hand. He shook his head. "Hell if I know."

"You said witches sometimes take the form of snakes, right?"

Tom didn't answer. He didn't want to think it. He couldn't. Witches weren't real. He didn't believe in magic. He didn't believe in any of that superstitious nonsense, and he wasn't going to start now. But he could think of no other way to explain the snake's strange behavior.

As if giving up waiting for his answer, Jessie glanced in the direction the horses had gone. "Will they be okay?"

Tom nodded. At least he had a reasonable answer for that question. "They'll head back to the barn. They know the way. They should be fine."

"And us?"

"We have a long walk home." He glanced around at the rough landscape—a landscape where mountain lions and bears prowled at night. But native wildlife wasn't what worried him. As long as the animals behaved the way they were supposed to behave and didn't disappear into thin air, he could handle them.

"What if that snake *was* a witch, Tom? A witch trying to keep us from learning the truth behind Roberto's and Joe's deaths?"

Tom squinted up at the sky. He had no answers. At least, none he was comfortable giving. "The only thing that's going to keep us from learning the truth is running out of daylight before we can find a safe spot to spend the night. Let's get looking."

JESSIE STOOD near the base of the cliff in the gathering darkness and checked her cell phone for the fiftieth time in the ten miles or so they'd walked. "The signal's here one second, then I lose it."

Tom nodded from his seat in a hollow dug into the cliff wall. Twilight glinted blue-black off his hair, his bronze skin blending with the shadows. "We are in the mountains."

She glanced at the snowcaps, blood red with the fading light of day. Cell phone trouble wasn't uncommon in the area, but she'd never had as much trouble as she'd had in the past few days. "My batteries are getting low, too." She stuffed the useless phone in her pocket and shivered.

"You're cold. Come here." Something glistened in his eyes—heat, intensity. He gestured to the spot next to him.

Tension trilled along her nerves. When she was a girl, she dreamed of sitting beside him in an intimate setting like this. Cuddling close to his lithe body. Soaking up his heat. Tonight her mouth went dry at the prospect. It made her feel too vulnerable—and she couldn't afford vulnerable. "I'm okay."

"What are you going to do? Stand all night? And it's going to get colder now that the sun is setting."

He was right. She was freezing. She was an adult now, not a girl with a crush. Sitting next to Tom shouldn't be a big deal. She sat.

He slipped an arm around her shoulders. Heat radiated from him. His clean, honest scent wrapped around her, enveloping her senses. The solid feel of his body pressed against the length of her side.

A laugh shook her and bubbled from her lips.

"What is so funny?"

"Nothing."

"What?"

"Something from when I was a kid."

He peered at her as if waiting for more of an explanation.

She shook her head, careful not to meet his gaze. "You don't want to know."

"What do you mean? I'd love to know." His voice tickled low and intimate in her ear.

Another laugh trembled through her chest despite herself, this time cut with an edge of nervousness. "I just had a crush on you. That's all. It's kind of funny now."

"A crush?"

She could feel him smile. She tried to dismiss her admission with a wave of her hand. "You know, teenage girls."

"No, I don't. But I did know you. You were cute as hell."

She laughed and looked at him out of the corner of her eye. "Really? I figured I was probably more of a pest back then than anything."

"No. You were easy to talk to. Down to earth. And so sweet. But I must admit, I like the adult version more."

A flush of heat rushed through her bloodstream. She looked out at the mountains.

"So how did you come to be an FBI agent?"

She exhaled with relief. A safe topic. One she could handle. She gave him a grateful smile. "I was always interested in law enforcement, ever since I was young. My dad hated the idea."

"Like he hated baseball?"

"Yeah. I think he would have hated anything I decided I wanted."

"I've done legal work for your father, writing contracts, that sort of thing. He's a hard man to please. It must have been tough growing up with him."

She nodded. "It was tough, but not as tough as not having a family, I'll bet."

Tom shrugged. "Did your mother encourage you?"

"Not really. I don't think she was able to. She was working as hard as I was to earn my dad's approval."

"That's sad."

"I had a great nanny."

"But a nanny isn't family."

"You only say that because you haven't met Guadalupe." She laughed again. This time it felt good. "She's as fierce as a bear and as tender as a flower, that's what her son says when he teases her."

"Ah, so she's the one you take after."

Jessie smiled. She liked that thought. "Lupe raised me. She still works for my parents. They probably couldn't function without her."

"Is she proud of how far you've gotten?"

"Yeah. She worries about me. But she knows it's what I have to do. It's how I have to prove myself."

"It must be tough for a woman in a male-dominated field."

It was tough. Every step of the way she had to be twice as good as the male special agents to get a fraction of the respect. Any mistake, any sign of vulnerability, and she would lose all the ground she'd gained. "I do okay."

"From what I've seen you do better than okay."

Warmth draped her like a blanket. His kind words, his confidence in her…she hadn't gotten much of that in her life. Certainly not from a man. But Tom seemed to know just what to say to build her up. "Thanks."

"I mean it, Jessie. You've grown into an incredible woman."

Her throat tightened. She knew she shouldn't look at him. She should focus on the mountains, the dark shapes of juniper—anything. She peered into his eyes.

Tom's gaze met hers and for a moment she forgot to

breathe. Her pulse throbbed in her ears. Awareness shimmered through her blood like champagne bubbles.

He leaned closer. His scent wrapped around her, teasing her, tempting her, calling her. He lowered his mouth. His lips teased hers, gentle at first, then beseeching, demanding.

She wrapped her arms around his neck, kissing him back, savoring the flavor of him, the scent, the heat. God, she wanted him. She had for so long. Wanted him. *Needed* him.

Something inside her bristled. She pulled back.

"You okay?" His brows dipped with concern.

"I'm fine. I just…can't."

"Kiss me?"

"This is a big case for me. I have to focus. I can't deal with this kind of distraction." This kind of vulnerability. She swallowed into a tight throat.

Tom leaned his head back against the rock behind them. "I understand. I even agree. We have to do our best for Roberto and Joe and their families." His words seemed sincere, yet she heard a note of regret in his voice, a note of longing.

And an answering longing ached in her chest.

Chapter Seven

Tom stared at the door of Jessie's hotel room, fist poised to knock. They'd only been apart for a day since returning from the desert and yet the anticipation of seeing her again twisted his gut into knots. The more time he spent with her, the more he wanted to spend talking to her, kissing her, touching her.

Shaking his head, he dropped his arm to his side. Jessie had been right when she'd called a stop to their kiss in the desert. They needed to focus on a murder case, not on the attraction buzzing between them.

The doorknob clattered. Jessie pulled the door open and looked up at him, startled.

Tom gave her what he hoped was an all-business smile. "I was just about to knock."

She laughed. "I was on my way to meet you in the lobby."

Silence hung between them, heavy, charged.

Jessie broke it. "I have something I have to tell you. And you're not going to like it."

"What?"

"The Bureau sent evidence techs out to the spot where we found the skeleton. I'm afraid they had to forge a road to get out there."

Tom flinched. He could just imagine the damage to vegetation and animal life, not to mention future erosion. The pueblo had kept that land unspoiled for generations.

"I tried to get them to use a helicopter, but they couldn't justify the cost. And they had to get vehicles out there somehow. It was the only way they could collect everything."

He nodded reluctantly. "What did they find?"

The apology in Jessie's eyes sparked to excitement. "A bullet. They expedited the analysis, and the preliminary ballistics report shows it's a probable match to the bullet that killed Joe Cordova."

He sucked in a breath. "So the murders are connected. Same weapon, nearly the same area. How long do they think the body was out there?"

"Hard to tell. Years."

"Do they have an ID yet?"

"No. The lab expects to know more with time, but the preliminary examination of the body shows he's a white male, probably in his mid-twenties."

A weight descended into Tom's gut. "So you want to talk to Ashley Donaldson?"

Jessie pressed her lips together and gave a solemn nod. "I need to find out if there's a connection between her amulet and the one we found on the skeleton."

"I'll go with you." A bad feeling hung in the back of his mind like gathering storm clouds. "But first I'll call Luke. If there is a connection, he should be with Ashley."

It didn't take long to call Luke and drive out to his home on the edge of pueblo land. Soon they were standing in Luke's living room.

"You wanted to talk to me?" Ashley asked, her hazel eyes frightened, as if she could sense bad news hanging in the air. Luke moved close behind her and she reached for his hand. "What is it, Special Agent? Just spit it out. Please."

Beside Tom, Jessie took a deep breath, as if searching for a way to soften the blow.

Tom knew from experience there was no way.

Apparently coming to that conclusion, Jessie looked straight into Ashley's eyes. "We found a body in the desert. A skeleton. There was an amulet around its neck that matches yours."

Ashley's hand flew to the stone at her throat. "Joe told me my father wore a matching amulet. He gave this one to my mother as a symbol of their love."

Tom flinched inwardly. He was afraid there was a connection. Afraid for Ashley. She didn't need more tragedy piled on top of losing Joe, a man he knew had meant a lot to her.

"Are you in contact with your father?" Jessie continued in a steady voice.

Ashley reached back and gripped Luke's hand. "He disappeared when I was a baby. His name was Brian Thompson. You think it's him in the desert, don't you? You think he's dead."

"We don't know," Jessie said.

Ashley's eyes filled with tears. "I always hoped to find him someday. To know him. But if the skeleton is him…"

Luke gathered her into his arms, holding her, supporting her. Ashley clung to him.

Tom's throat closed. Ashley was lucky to have Luke with her. Supporting her. Loving her. Helping her through whatever tragedies they had to confront.

Tom watched Jessie, her businesslike yet tender manner. Her strength. The sweetness she'd never lost. Longing hollowed out his chest.

"I know this is hard, Ashley," Jessie said. "But you can help."

Ashley blinked back tears. "How?"

Jessie reached into her jacket pocket and pulled out two clear plastic tubes with cotton swabs inside. "I need to rub these swabs on the insides of your cheeks to get a DNA sample. If the lab can compare your DNA with the mitochondrial DNA from the bone marrow—"

"You can tell whether the body you found is my father."

"Yes."

Ashley set her quivering chin and nodded. "I'll do it. I have to know."

Jessie took the DNA samples and sealed, dated and initialed the tubes. "Thank you, Ashley."

Ashley gripped Luke's hand. "Will you tell me the results?"

"As soon as I know them."

JESSIE'S MIND WHIRLED as they drove from Luke's house back to Santa Fe. Telling Ashley her father might very well be dead was one of the worst things she'd had to do in her short career. Having Tom by her side had made it bearable. He'd hardly said a word, but she'd felt his steadiness, his confidence in her, his compassion through the entire exchange. And she was profoundly grateful.

She glanced at his profile as he piloted his truck through the winding streets of Santa Fe on the way to Canyon Road and the Milagro Gallery. "Thanks for going with me."

He nodded. "It's hard, telling a family member tragic news."

"Yes."

"You did a great job."

Warmth suffused her. She wasn't used to praise, and it made her feel almost as clumsy and awkward as criticism.

Tom smiled. "I mean it. If there's such a thing as bedside manner in law enforcement, you have it. You're a natural."

A shimmer traveled down her spine. She took a deep breath and struggled to bring her feelings under control. Yet she couldn't get over how much easier the job seemed with the glow of Tom's confidence warming her. "Are you sure Charlotte's at the gallery?"

"That's what her grandmother said." He swung the pickup into the parking lot and an empty space.

They exited the truck, climbed the stairs and entered the front door. Inside, the place seemed deserted. The sounds of guitars and haunting flutes played on the sound system, but neither Rico nor his assistant emerged to greet them. And she didn't see Charlotte anywhere. Yet Jessie couldn't shake an uneasy sensation traveling over her skin, as if they were being watched. She was about to check the area screened by deer hides when an unfamiliar deep voice rose over the music. "You're crazy, you know that? As nuts as that grandmother of yours."

Jessie stepped close to a deer hide panel and strained to hear. Tom did the same.

"There's a lot of wisdom in the old ways," a woman's voice said quietly.

At the sound of the feminine voice, Tom mouthed Charlotte's name.

Jessie nodded and strained to hear over the music.

"You shouldn't go misleading the FBI with your wild tales." The man's voice again.

"I didn't tell wild tales. I merely suggested she look in the areas Joe painted."

"A suggestion based on some kind of vision you had? In my book, that's a wild tale."

Jessie had heard enough. She cleared her throat and slipped into the alcove. "Excuse me."

Charlotte jumped.

The potter who had been trying to convince Rico to show his artwork, Raul Estevez, stood next to her, a scowl on his face. "I was just leaving."

"Stay. You can fill me in on these visions you were talking about." Jessie felt Tom slip in beside her. She kept her focus trained on Charlotte and Raul.

Raul held his hands up in front of him. "I'm not the one with visions. You'll have to talk to Charlotte about that nonsense. I have to find Soto." He rushed out of the alcove.

Jessie let him go. She didn't want him to hear what she had to say anyway. "We found a body out there, Charlotte. It was skeletonized."

Charlotte nodded, as if she'd expected it. As if she knew.

Jessie narrowed her eyes on the taller, dark-eyed beauty. "Tell me about your visions."

"They aren't visions."

"What are they?"

"Joe was an amazing artist. In his paintings, his images always carried more than one meaning."

"Such as?"

"It depends on the image. Let me show you." She stepped aside and gestured to the lone Joe Cordova painting.

"I see the area near the spring," Jessie said, squinting at the painting as if that would help her see more. "I see the vein of orange rock in the canyon wall."

"And do you see this?" Charlotte stretched out an elegantly tapered finger and pointed to a detail in the painting. There at the spot where the arroyo had cut into the *bajada* at the base of the cliff—right in the spot where they'd found the skeleton—were fine white lines etched in the paint.

Tom leaned close. "It looks like the sun-bleached juniper branches you find all over the desert. How did you know those lines represented human bones?"

"I didn't. I was just looking for another meaning Joe might have intended. There are no visions. No magic."

"So that was just Raul's superstition?"

"Exactly."

Jessie nodded. Next to her Tom was totally still, as if weighing Charlotte's explanation.

Jessie looked back to the painting. Joe had to have known about the skeleton to have included it. Is that why he'd painted the area over and over? To let people know a murder had taken place there? To alert someone as perceptive as Charlotte to the crime? But if he'd wanted people to know about the body, why hadn't he simply gone to the police? Why be cryptic about it? And who in the world had shot Joe with the same gun that had killed the man in the desert? Had the murderer shot Joe when he realized what clues the painter was leaving in his artwork? That would explain the theft of Joe's paintings—if the theft was related.

There were too many questions. Jessie needed answers. But before she could continue to prod Charlotte Reyna, her cell phone bleated over the guitar and flutes. She excused herself, snatched it from her belt, flipped it open and punched the talk button. "Special Agent Gardner."

"Jessica." Her father's voice boomed in her ear. "Where are you?"

Her stomach tensed the way it always did at her father's voice. "What is it, Dad?"

"You need to pick up your mother."

"Mom? Why? Did something happen?"

"Something happened, all right. And I'm not wasting my time dealing with it this time."

"This time?" Now she was really confused. "What's going on?"

"She's at that damn casino again. She's in trouble with the law. If you can't bother yourself to give me a little information, the least you can do is use your influence to get your mother out of this mess."

Her mother was a civic leader in Santa Fe. A belle of upper-crust society. Jessie couldn't imagine what her father was talking about. "How is she in trouble with the law?"

"Don't ask questions. Just do something for your family for once in your life and straighten this out. That is, if you even can." The phone went dead.

The hard edge in her father's voice rang in her ears even after he hung up, and once again she was that little girl who couldn't do anything right. That little girl who was never good enough.

She could feel Tom looking at her, waiting for her to tell him what the call was about. But she couldn't bear to return his gaze. She stared down at her hands gripping the cell phone. "Will you drive me to the Sena Casino?"

"Of course."

Chapter Eight

Tom followed Jessie into the casino. Even though she'd announced on the drive that she would take care of the problem alone, he couldn't desert her. She was upset, that much was obvious. And he couldn't help but feel she needed him, even if she didn't want to admit it.

He'd been about to confront Charlotte when Jessie's cell phone had interrupted. The artist was hiding something. He was sure of it. And for the life of him, he couldn't figure out what. But whatever it was, it would have to wait. Jessie needed him now. And he sure as hell wasn't going to let her down.

Bells and electronic bleeps jangled in his ears as they skirted the rows of slot machines and blackjack tables on their way to the security office. The office door stood ajar, bright light streaming out into the neon-lit dim. The casino manager, Miguel Silva, and Fred Gonzales peered at them as they stepped inside. A smug smile pulled back from yellowed teeth as Gonzales leered at Jessie. "If it isn't the little fibbie."

Tom wanted to belt him. "What's going on here, Gonzales?"

The tribal cop stepped to the side, revealing Jessie's mother sitting in the center of the office. Usually coiffed and buffed to within an inch of becoming the poster child for rich men's wives, Kathleen Paxton looked like the product of an all-night bender and a lot of crying. Dark moons of mascara puddled under her eyes. Her lipstick bled out from her lips in a red smear. And her body wove slightly as if she was having trouble balancing in her chair.

"Mom." Jessie raced to her mother's side. Bending, she gave her mom a hug.

Her mother didn't hug her back. "Where's your father? I asked your father to come." She slurred the words.

Tom bristled. Obviously the woman was drunk. But that was no excuse for treating her daughter that way. Especially a daughter who had raced to her side to help. A daughter as special as Jessie.

"Dad called me. He asked me to come."

Kathleen's face twisted with disappointment. "Why would he do that?"

"Because I'm a federal officer. He thought I could help."

Kathleen shook her head so hard she nearly fell off her chair. "No. He didn't come because he doesn't care."

Jessie touched a tender hand to her mother's shoulder. "I care, Mom. What happened?"

Kathleen glanced up at Gonzales. "He brought me in here. Why don't you ask him?"

Jessie looked at Gonzales and Miguel Silva in turn.

Gonzales grinned, obviously enjoying the moment. The ass.

Tom clenched his fists. What he wouldn't give to knock that smile off the tribal cop's face.

"Guess your mother needed more gambling money. Decided she'd try to sell stolen goods to Miguel here to get it." Gonzales chuckled.

"What kind of stolen goods?" Tom asked.

"A painting."

"A painting?" A bad feeling crept up Tom's spine. "What painting?"

"That's the interesting part." Gonzales stepped aside. Leaning against the stark white wall of the office was a colorful depiction of the canyon Jessie and Tom had visited two days before. "She had it in her car."

Jessie glanced at Tom. Neither had to point out the painting was one of Joe Cordova's.

"She was trying to push it on me to settle her gambling debts." Miguel Silva gave Tom a self-satisfied nod, his long, thin ponytail snaking over his shoulder, the office's fluorescent lighting glinting off his balding head. "Good thing Fred was here and saw what she was trying to do. The casino has a reputation to uphold. We aren't a pawn shop. And we certainly don't deal in stolen merchandise."

Tom frowned. "That's not what I heard." Luke had told him a much different story. And although Luke and Ashley hadn't been able to prove Silva was pawning merchandise to settle gambling debts, it seemed their suspicions were right on.

Silva took a step forward, hands on hips, his sports coat pushed back and his gut pushed out. Apparently the man's best attempt at a threatening posture. "You heard nothing."

"Nothing except that this is the second Cordova painting you've come up with since his death."

"Who told you that? It's a lie." He turned a red face on Gonzales. "It's a lie, Fred. You know it."

Fred Gonzales smirked. "All I know is that I have a stolen painting here in Mrs. Gardner's possession."

"Have you checked with Rico Tafoya?" Tom asked.

"Is this indeed one of the paintings that was stolen from Milagro?"

"It's not from a gallery." Kathleen's voice slurred.

Jessie knelt to look her mother in the eye. "Where did you get the painting, Mom?"

A fresh flood of tears bathed Kathleen's cheeks.

"Mom?" Jessie said, her voice kind and patient. "Where did it come from?"

"Joe."

"Joe Cordova?"

"He gave it to me. Before he died. Joe cared about me." Another wave of tears. "He loved me."

Jessie's face went pale. "Did Daddy know about you and Joe?"

"He found the painting. He put it together. He was furious. That's why I'm afraid…"

"Of what?"

"I'm afraid Paxton might have done something. That he might have killed Joe to keep him away from me."

Jessie jerked backward, as if her mother had dealt her a physical blow.

Tom grasped her shoulder. Gently he pulled her to her feet and against his body, steadying her.

Kathleen sat back in her chair and watched them, a slight gleam in her eye. As if the thought of her husband's violence pleased her in some way. As if it meant he cared.

Tom felt sick.

Jessie looked down at her mother. "Roberto Sanchez was found with the murder weapon. He claimed Joe's killer paid him to retrieve it. Did Daddy know Sanchez?"

"Roberto used to clean at Rico Tafoya's gallery."

Jessie nodded. "But Daddy wouldn't have been friendly with a janitor. I can't imagine him even noticing Roberto was alive."

"He didn't notice Roberto. I did."

Tom circled an arm around Jessie. He wished she didn't have to hear this, didn't have to know the sordid truth. But wishing things were different changed nothing. The best he could do was to be there for her. To support her.

Jessie narrowed her eyes on her mother. "You had an affair with Roberto, too?"

"Not an affair. He was a nice man. I talked to him. Flirted with him. No one else was paying attention to me."

"And Daddy saw you flirting."

"He was angry. Jealous." Again, Kathleen's eyes sparkled. This time, she even had the gall to smile. "Don't look at me that way. I only started up with Joe and Roberto because Paxton spent all his time at that house."

"House? What house, Mom?"

"Paxton has a love nest in the mountains."

Jessie exhaled. She seemed to be absorbing all this with little problem. But Tom wasn't fooled. He could feel the tremor in her body. The rigid stress of each muscle. Jessie was strong, but even the strong could break.

"That's enough," Tom said. He glared at Gonzales. "You have nothing to hold Mrs. Gardner. We're taking her home."

"You expect me to believe her word that the painting wasn't stolen?"

"You have no reason not to. If you come up with evidence, you know where to find her. In the meantime, you might want to think about charging Silva here for turning his casino into a pawn shop."

THE FEW TIMES Tom had written contracts for Paxton Gardner, he'd met the man in his Santa Fe offices. He'd never been to the man's home. And as he glanced around the formal living room, waiting for Jessie to settle her mother into bed, he couldn't help wishing he was anywhere else.

It wasn't that the place was uncomfortable. What bothered him was that it was too comfortable. Handwoven rugs of extraordinary richness draped the hand-painted-tile floor. Extraordinary Native American paintings adorned the walls. And what looked like ancient Anasazi pottery, or at least very good copies, lined shelves and clustered on tables. The history of his people bought, sold and collected for a rich white man's pleasure.

He forced his hands to unfold from their fists and sank into one of the plush chairs. He knew he shouldn't let Paxton Gardner's penchant for collecting Native American art bother him. A lot of people liked to collect the beautiful pieces, including Tom himself. And his friend Rico had built a business around selling artwork and providing a living for dozens of artists. But somehow Paxton Gardner was different. Tom couldn't help feeling the man collected art not because of its beauty, but because of its value. As if the pueblo people's culture and history was worth nothing more than dollars. And that was a sentiment that made his blood bubble with anger.

He took a deep breath and tried to focus on the hum of voices in the hall. Jessie talking to the sweet, motherly woman who had once been her nanny. The voices stopped. When he looked up, Jessie was peering at him from the doorway. She looked tired, her face pale. "Mom's finally asleep. Lupe said she'd listen for her, take care of her if she woke up."

Tom's anger faded, his resentment toward Paxton Gardner fading with it. Somehow when Jessie was in the room, everything changed. From the first time he'd met her, she'd made him forget he was a dirt-poor Indian working as a stock boy in a grocery store. Around her, he'd felt he was capable of becoming anything he wanted to be. Even now that he was a lawyer, her presence had the same effect. Whenever she looked at him, he found himself discovering new strengths and weighing new possibilities. Whenever she was near him, he felt he could win any battle. That he could change the world.

He thrust himself up from the chair and crossed the room to her. Slipping an arm around her delicate shoulders, he pulled her close. "You look like you've had enough for one day. You've done what you can to take care of your mom. Now it's time to let me take care of you."

JESSIE LEANED BACK in the soft comfort of Tom's couch and dragged in a deep breath. She was still shaking from the episode with her mother, but she'd made it without breaking down. A miracle. Maybe she was stronger than she'd thought. Or maybe knowing that Tom was there with her gave her that strength. Whatever it was, she'd gotten her mother home and poured her into bed. And when Lupe had insisted she and her son would be happy to watch over Kathleen, Jessie had finally let Tom talk her into coming back to his house. Maybe not smart, but she hadn't wanted to be alone. Not tonight.

He sat next to her and handed her a glass of water. "Are you okay?"

She nodded.

"Everything you said about Guadalupe was true. I'm glad I got to meet her. She's an impressive woman. And she's obviously very proud of you."

Jessie's lower lip quivered slightly before she regained control. He knew just what to say, what she needed to hear. But at the same time, his words were sincere. Honest. "What if it's true, Tom? What if my father killed Joe and Roberto?"

"Your mother was guessing."

"I know. But what if she's right?"

"He'll go to prison, and you'll go on."

She knew he was right. People faced tragedy all the time and somehow they picked up and went on. She would, too. "He came to see me the day after Roberto was killed. He wanted information about the case."

"That isn't proof that he has anything to do with it."

"Maybe not. But I have a bad feeling about it."

He slipped his hand behind her neck and rubbed the muscles in her shoulders. "Have you thought about asking to be removed from the case?"

She bristled in spite of herself.

"I know you don't want to give up, and that it might not be great for your career, but I think you should consider it. For your own sake."

Truth was, he was right. She should consider it. But she didn't want to go there. Not unless she was forced to. "If I find evidence my dad was involved, I'll ask to be removed."

"Fair enough." He gently spun her on the couch so that her back was to him and began massaging her tense muscles. "We'll start working on that tomorrow. Tonight, you need to recover. You've had quite a shock."

He was right. She'd worry about the case tomorrow. Tonight she wanted only to feel Tom's fingers kneading her muscles and to know he was here with her.

Tom Lahi was an amazing man, that was for certain. All she had to do was think of the way he'd stepped in to defend her mother to feel more in awe of him than she ever had. And the most amazing thing of all was how good he made her feel about herself. How strong and capable. He didn't use her vulnerability against her. He built her up, supported her, had confidence in her. She wanted that. She wanted him. And she was tired of denying what she wanted.

Leaning back against him, she met his eyes and parted her lips.

He lowered his mouth to hers. He kissed her hungrily, needily. As if he couldn't get enough of her. As if she gave him the same strength, the same sustenance that he gave her. Finally he broke away from her and looked into her eyes. "Is this what you want?"

"Yes." Her voice came out in a whisper, but with all the passion and need of a shout.

Tom rose from the couch. Holding her hand, he led her to the bedroom. He lit a candle, then turned back to her, the flame reflecting in his dark eyes.

She shrugged out of her jacket and freed herself from her shoulder holster as he stripped off his shirt. But before she could unbutton her blouse, he caught her hands. "I want to undress you." He lowered her hands to her sides.

She stood perfectly still as he slipped each button free and parted the silky blouse to reveal her bra. He skimmed the blouse off her arms and let it fall to the floor with the jumble of already divested clothing. Then he circled her with his arms and unfastened her bra.

Her breasts hung free and heavy, her nipples puckering under his gaze.

He sucked in a breath.

She closed her eyes as his hands cupped her, as the warm moisture of his mouth kissed and suckled and claimed. She moved her hands up to his bare shoulders. She wanted him to touch all of her, to kiss all of her, to claim all of her. A moan echoed from her throat.

He trailed kisses down her stomach. Unfastening her

belt, he pushed slacks and panties over her hips and down her legs. After slipping off shoes and socks, he showered kisses back up her legs until he reached the tender spot between her thighs.

His first kiss shuddered through her. His second sent her spinning close to the edge.

She dug her fingers into his shoulders and held on.

He kissed and teased and dipped inside her until her knees felt weak. Then he picked her up and carried her to the bed.

He set her on top of the comforter, the cotton cool against her skin. Then he stood back, looking at her.

A tinge of unease niggled at her. She pressed her thighs together.

"No." He touched her legs and gently moved them apart again, exposing the most vulnerable part of her. "You're so beautiful. I want to see you."

Her skin heated as his gaze moved over her, as powerful as a touch, as intimate as a kiss. She wanted him inside her. She wanted to join with him, to be part of him. But she lay there, unmoving. Soaking in the heat of his gaze. Letting it stoke her desire. Her need.

Still looking at her, he unbuckled his belt and slid jeans and briefs down powerful legs, exposing lithe lines of hard muscle beneath bronzed skin. His erection jutted free.

Warmth and wetness rushed between her legs. She reached up for him and pulled him to her.

He penetrated her slowly, stretching her, filling her. He fit her perfectly, and her womb contracted with the feel of him, the want of him. He settled into a rhythm, each thrust going deeper, taking her higher. His lips found hers. He plundered her mouth with his tongue. Cradling her head, he deepened the kiss as he thrust into her, until they truly were part of each other, they truly were one.

Pleasure broke over her in waves, contracting and ebbing. She whispered his name, her voice stolen by the power, the passion. And when she finally felt his body tense with his own release, she knew neither of them would ever be the same.

Chapter Nine

Jessie curled into Tom's embrace. She'd never felt so warm, so sated. She wanted to stay in his arms forever. She closed her eyes, even though she could already hear the birds beginning to twitter outside. Soon the sun would start illuminating the sky and she would have to turn her mind to other things. But right now she wanted to spend every moment they had left soaking in the sense of belonging she felt in Tom's arms.

A cell phone's shrill ring slashed her thoughts.

Tom jolted awake and scrambled out of bed. Groping through the mixed jumble of clothing on the floor, he produced a cell phone and flipped it open. "Lahi." He frowned into the phone. "Just a second." Reaching across the bed, he handed the phone to Jessie. "Sorry. I thought it was mine."

Jessie took the phone and held it to her ear. "Special Agent Gardner."

"Jessica, why is Tom Lahi answering your phone at this hour?"

Her father. Cold dread pooled in the pit of her stomach.

"Where are you right now?" he barked.

"Does it matter?"

"I thought you were going to take care of your mother, not just drop her here with the servants."

"I put Mom to bed. Lupe encouraged me to go."

"So she told me. Though why you'd let a servant tell you what to do is beyond me. Did she tell you to sleep with that Indian lawyer, too?"

Jessie closed her eyes. She refused to answer, refused to accept this kind of abuse. "I have to go." She punched the end button and let the phone fall onto the sheets. Opening her eyes, she looked at Tom.

Concern tightened his lips and furrowed his brow. "Are you okay?"

"He's not happy we're together."

He nodded. "Not surprising. I'm the hired help, you know."

That was right. Tom had done legal work for her father. Her heart stuttered. "Oh, shit."

"What?"

How had she made this kind of mistake? "I've jeopardized the entire case, my entire career."

Tom reached out for her, alarmed. "How? What happened?"

"You're my dad's lawyer."

Understanding dawned in Tom's eyes. He rubbed a hand over his face. "Oh, Jessie. I'm sorry. I've only written a few contracts for him. I never even thought that being with you could be construed as a conflict of interest."

"If my dad is responsible for Joe's and Roberto's deaths, I've just crippled the case against him."

"We don't know that he's responsible."

"But if he is, my career is over. Yours, too. He'll see to it. And he might even be able to duck murder charges."

Tom reached for her.

But she couldn't return to his arms. Not now. She scrambled out of bed. As much as she wanted his touch, as much as she wanted to feel she wasn't alone in this mess, she couldn't pull him in deeper. "It was a mistake, me staying here with you. The whole thing was a mistake."

"A mistake? It wasn't a mistake, damn it." Moonlight filtering through the window highlighted his naked skin, his powerful body, his piercing eyes. "We've been destined to get together since we were kids, Jessie. You know it, and I know it. Don't let your father erase what we've found. What has always been between us."

She swallowed into a dry throat and looked away. "I'm not dragging you down with me, Tom."

"I'm not afraid of your father."

No. Of course he wasn't. Tom wasn't afraid of anything. Hadn't he taken on the federal government more than once to defend his people? Hadn't he been willing to take on the supernatural to defend her? And by dragging him into this situation, hadn't she caused him to be vulnerable to her father's power? "I'm not going to let my father get you disbarred, Tom."

"He won't get me disbarred."

"You don't know that. He's a powerful man."

"Because he's rich?"

"Yes. And because he's ruthless."

"I can be ruthless, too, when it comes to fighting for justice. And for the woman I've fallen in love with."

Her heart stilled in her chest.

"Do you love me, Jessie?"

She did. She always had. With her whole heart, her whole mind, her whole being. "It doesn't matter."

"It matters more than anything else in life."

"No." She couldn't talk to Tom now. She couldn't look at him. Seeing the rippling muscles under naked skin, being so close she could reach out and touch him, only made her long to run into his arms. To let him hold her and protect her. And she couldn't do that. Not now.

Now she had to stand on her own. If there was any time for her to prove her mettle, this was it.

She picked up her bra and panties from the clothes on the floor.

"Where are you going?"

"To my hotel. I need to be alone to figure things out. To think. Just for a little while. Will you give me that, Tom? Please?"

The fierceness didn't fade from his eyes, but he finally offered a reluctant nod. "Only a few hours. Then I'm going to be by your side whether you want me there or not. Your father be damned."

"Tom—"

"You don't have a choice, Jessie. You're stuck with me."

A cold fear crawled up her spine and spread over her skin. She didn't doubt Tom's words. Not for a moment. And if he wouldn't let her shield him from her father, there was only one alternative left.

JESSIE SLAMMED THE DOOR of her SUV and stared at the small adobe house that dug into the side of the mountain. Her father's love nest. She braced herself for the wave of anger she expected to overtake her at the thought of her father's possible crimes, but it never came. Had she entirely given up on him? Given up pleasing him? Given up loving him?

She took a deep breath, trying to quell the ache in her chest. She'd spent her whole life trying to prove herself to her father. But it was impossible. She could never win his approval. She had only to look at her mother's sad life to know that. Why hadn't she recognized it before?

Tom.

She'd never had to prove herself to him. Unlike her

father and her colleagues in law enforcement, Tom had accepted her from the first. He'd always believed she was worthy.

The ache in her chest deepened until it throbbed through her whole body. She couldn't let her father destroy Tom's career, the good work to which he'd devoted his life. And that's why she was here. To find evidence proving her case. To put her father in prison. And once she did that, she'd drive back down that winding road and find Tom, tell him what was in her heart and pray he'd take her back into his arms and never let her go.

She forced her feet to move forward. Skirting a coyote fence screening the side yard, she walked to the front door and let herself in with the key her mother had given her.

The house was dark, and it took a few seconds for her eyes to adjust after the bright sun outside. But when they did, it was clear she wasn't looking at a cozy love nest.

Stacks of taped cardboard boxes and wood crates crowded the main room. At the far end, they nearly reached the beamed ceiling. And nowhere was there a stick of furniture or any sign that someone lived here. The place looked like a storehouse.

She stepped deeper into the room. Silence hung in her ears and caused a nervous tremor to slink up her spine. The scent of cardboard and dust tickled her nose…along with the faint scent of smoke.

She moved in the direction of the scent. It seemed to be coming from outside. She walked to the back door and pulled it open. Fenced on only one side, the yard was bare except for a small smoldering pile in its center. She stepped closer. Grabbing a stick of juniper, she stirred the blackened pile. Under the ash, color peeked out at her. Rich browns and oranges and greens in broad strokes… The canyon in the desert… Joe's paintings.

A sound reached her, the soft crunch of a footstep. She looked up just as a gray-brown streak disappeared around the edge of the fence.

She withdrew her Glock and circled the fire. Peering around the fence, she looked for the animal, but nothing was there. A cold feeling sank into her bones just as something heavy crashed down on her skull.

THE WITCH looked down at Jessica's limp form in the dust. How had it come to this?

He hadn't wanted to hurt her. Even when he'd shot at her in the desert, he'd only wanted to frighten her. To make her back off. Now he couldn't let her tell what she'd seen in the house. Couldn't let her describe the burning pile of Joe Cordova's paintings. Someone might put the pieces together. Someone might figure out the truth.

Didn't he feel a presence already? Someone seeing too much, knowing too much. If Jessica lived, she would bring the whole FBI down on him. They'd find out everything. And all his years of work wouldn't matter a damn. It would all be over.

He grasped her under the armpits and dragged her back into the house, bracing himself for what he must do. There was no other way. It was a choice between him and Jessica.

Jessica had to die.

TOM WATCHED the trail of smoke rise from the mountain through his truck's dusty windshield. He pushed the accelerator to the floor, willing the old truck to move faster up the incline.

When he'd shown up at Jessie's hotel room door

after a few hours of driving around and berating himself for not recognizing the position he'd put her in, she'd been gone. And it hadn't taken him long to figure out where she would go.

The smoke ahead seemed to grow thicker. Fear drummed in his veins. He could only pray something bad hadn't happened to her. He could only pray he wasn't too late.

The pickup skidded on loose gravel. The truck's engine wheezed, but the tires kept moving, climbing the road until he reached the adobe house. He slid to a stop next to Jessie's SUV and bolted from his vehicle.

Flames licked from one of the windows. Panic surged in Tom's blood. Jessie couldn't be inside, could she?

He raced for the door. The handle searing his palm, he yanked it open. A wave of smoke and heat gushed from the building. "Jessie!"

No answer.

Dragging in a deep breath, he plunged into the smoke. Heat scorched him. Smoke stung his eyes. He plunged on. He had to find her. If she was in here, she couldn't survive long. Not in the smoke, the heat. He had to get her out.

The room was dark, but through the haze he could see flame and the hulking shapes of boxes. He kicked one with his foot. Then another. Empty. Nothing but fuel for the fire. Kicking more boxes aside, he saw her.

She lay prone in the middle of the room. Her hair glowed with the light of nearby flame. Her face was pale as ash.

Tom gathered her in his arms and held her to his chest. Cradling her close, he made for the door. He stumbled outside, gasping for air. Moving a safe distance from the fire, he lowered her to the ground.

She didn't move.

No!

He tilted her head back and blew air into her mouth, into her lungs. He pressed his ear to her chest, straining to hear her heart. A light rhythm reached him, the beat of life, however faint. He closed his lips over hers again, breathing into her, trying to fuel her life with his breath.

She didn't move. Didn't breathe on her own.

He kept up the rhythm of mouth-to-mouth resuscitation. Helplessness washed over him, as thick and life-choking as the smoke. She couldn't die. He'd finally found her. The woman who called to his soul. The woman he wanted to form a family with, to grow old with, to love.

He'd begun to doubt there was good left in the world until he'd seen Jessie again. She'd given him strength. She'd made him feel his battle for justice wasn't hopeless. That with her by his side, he could take on any injustice and win. She'd opened his mind to the possibility of magic, of love.

A sound worked up his throat and hummed in his ears. A chant he recognized from when he was a child. A chant he sometimes still heard echoing from his neighbor's home. A healing chant. It bubbled up in him, as if fueled by something bigger than him, something more powerful, something he could no longer deny. As if his need, his love for Jessie had broken it loose, issued it forth. When his chant was finished, he bent low over her and whispered in her ear. "Jessie, I love you. I need you. Don't leave me."

Her breath caressed his cheek. A tremor shook her. Coughs racked her body.

"Jessie." Tom gathered her in his arms, holding her as she struggled to breathe.

Coughs subsiding, she looked up at him, her eyes filled with tears. "I think it was my father, Tom. There's a pile of canvases burning in the yard. Joe's canvases. I think he's behind the gallery thefts. And Joe's and Roberto's deaths. And…he tried to kill me."

Anger flooded him, but he held back. There would be time for anger, time for battle, time for justice. But now wasn't that time. Now was time to hold Jessie, to support her, to let her know how much he loved her and that he would always be there. "Jess, I'm so sorry."

"I worked all my life to win his respect. His approval. And now to think…"

He cradled her to his chest, soaking in the softness of her. The strength. "You deserve respect, Jessie. You've always had mine."

She smiled through her tears. "Thanks to you, I can see there's no need to work so hard to prove myself to people like my father—people who will never give me credit—not if I truly believe in myself. And I do."

"I love you, you know that?"

"I love you, too, Tom." She peered at him, eyes shining with determination, with growing strength. "I'm going to call my supervisor and ask him to take me off the case."

"And you're okay with that?"

"I'm okay. If I stay on the investigation, it would only taint the case against my father. But…"

"What is it?"

"I don't want my father to walk away. I want to make sure he pays for what he's done. And there's no telling when the FBI will assign a new special agent to the case or who it will be. And we certainly can't rely on Fred Gonzales to find the truth."

"What are you proposing?"

"Nothing. Not officially. But if you want to do a little investigating on your own, I certainly can't stop you." A smile lifted her beautiful lips.

The heat of her smile blazed hotter than the flames licking from the windows of the house.

His throat grew tight. He lowered his lips to hers. Her mouth was warm and smoky, and as he kissed her, she softened and opened to him, taking him deep. And when the kiss ended, he knew he had everything he'd longed for, everything he needed, right here in his arms. "Marry me, Jessie. Have children with me. I want us to be part of one another for the rest of our lives."

"I want that, too." She smiled, an open, defenseless, vulnerable smile. A smile filled with strength and possibility.

And Tom knew he'd finally found his life, his family. And that the rest of his days would be filled with the healing magic of love.

RICO
PATRICIA ROSEMOOR

Chapter One

Wind whistles through the slash in the rock wall behind her. Pulse skittering, she glances back once to make sure she's alone. She's been getting the feeling that someone knows...and now she fears that someone is watching as she wanders the high desert searching for clues.

Two dead already.

She doesn't want to be number three.

No sign of anyone...

She goes on.

The dry wash leads her into a narrow canyon guarded by towers of basalt. Passing giant boulders that tumbled down from the cliffs, she approaches a spring. The sun is high, the day hot. She kneels at the water's edge and cups a hand to capture some liquid. The cool water sliding down her throat gives her a moment to take in the beauty of the land. A million years ago, lava left a glowing streak of orange along the cliff wall.

If only the walls could talk.

Perhaps they could...

She listens hard, with every fiber she can muster. Nothing at first, but she centers herself and focuses un-

til male voices seem to murmur at her. The voices rise, as if in an argument, but they're garbled and she can't make out what they're saying.

Suddenly silence...

Is that a cry?

A gunshot?

Behind her, rock clacks against rock, the unexpected sound whirling her around. She sees no one, but the sense of not being alone returns. Another presence brushes by her, invisible, raising her flesh. Her heart thunders as she flies around in a circle trying to catch the elusive spirit.

Then she stops and listens again only to hear nothing but the rush of her own blood through her ears. Waiting for her heart to steady, she stands still and gathers her courage to finish what she set out to do.

She can *do this.*

She must before someone else gets killed.

Her gaze lifts to a ledge above. There. That's where she will head.

She takes a deep breath and but a single step when someone grips her shoulder from behind—

"AH-H!" Charlotte Reyna cried, heart threatening to pound right out of her chest as an earthly hand touched her. Barely seeing Joe Cordova's painting, she whirled around on her stool to meet gallery owner Rico Tafoya's simmering green gaze. "What do you think you're doing?" she demanded.

Rico's dark eyebrows lifted. "I was going to ask the same of you. It's after hours. The gallery is closed for business. The doors have been locked for nearly half an hour. Want to explain how you got in?"

Charlotte flushed but couldn't feel guilty. She was, after all, trying to get information that would help catch a murderer. Had she really been lost in her journey for so long? Amazing that Rico hadn't discovered her before this, though she was at a place in the long gallery divided by hand-worked deer hide panels.

She said, "I guess I just didn't leave when the others did."

"Then how about explaining what you're doing here."

Rico leaned a shoulder against a nearby pillar. His posture might be casual, but she wasn't fooled. His stance was as deliberate as everything else in his life, starting with the way he used his stunning good looks.

His long black hair was pulled back from a rugged tanned face in a careful braid lashed with a leather thong and decorated with a single raven's feather. His clothing was black, too—shirt, pants and boots. And he'd chosen a few pieces of pawn—a single earring, ring, belt buckle and bracelet—silver inlaid with green turquoise the exact shade of his pale green eyes. She knew that professionally Rico meant to play up the part of his tricultural heritage he personally ignored. He knew what it took to be a successful mestizo gallery owner selling Native American works in Santa Fe.

Charlotte chose to tell him something that would be the truth and yet not reveal too much. "I needed to see Joe's painting once more." Sadly, his paintings were all that were left of him.

"Apparently. The question is why."

"Inspiration," she hedged. It was the truth if the rest of her statement wasn't. "I like to study other artists before I begin a new painting of my own. Joe has been quite an influence on me."

"You were in a trance."

"I get lost in art."

"Especially in Joe's art," Rico observed. "This isn't the first time I've caught you so...involved. Want to tell me what's going on?"

"I told you—"

"A lie," he finished. "Your being here has something to do with Joe's murder, right?"

"His murder is The People's loss."

"Which people?"

"Our people. Pueblo."

"They're not our people. Not mine, not yours. We're mixed breeds, both of us. Your mother took you away to her Anglo world when you were too young to be attached. I walked away from pueblo life more than a decade ago because I wanted something better."

"You act as if you can deny your heritage."

"And you're just playing at it. When you get tired of living in a couple of small rooms and eating Indian tacos, you'll go back East to your real life."

Upstate New York held no promise for her. New Mexico had always called to her, prodding her to come home.

"This is my life now." Intending to leave, Charlotte rose from the stool and heard a tinkle as though something had dropped to the ground.

"You didn't answer my question," Rico said, distracting her.

"Which one?" she asked. "You're full of them tonight."

"How about we get right down to it. I know you've given a couple of clues about Joe's murder to Jessie Gardner for the FBI investigation. The question is... how? You find them in Joe's paintings?"

"You wouldn't believe me."

Perturbed by Rico's questioning, Charlotte started to leave. He caught hold of her arm and kept her there. He wasn't hurting her, but the warmth and strength of his long fingers made her uncomfortable. Her pulse accelerated and his gaze sharpened, making her feel as if Rico could look right through her. The escalating tension between them was palpable.

"Try me," he said. "What do you see in the paintings?"

"Not in them exactly," she said, despite her resolve not to involve him. "Through them."

"Explain."

Charlotte thought about pushing her way out of the gallery. Rico wouldn't really force her to do anything, not even to stay to answer his questions. And this wasn't the same Rico she remembered from their childhood—a boy who'd had a wild imagination and who'd stood up for the underdog, often her. But he was still friends with Tom Lahi and Luke Cordova. Maybe she shouldn't underestimate his interest in what had been happening to her.

"All right, I'll tell you. I've found a way to journey *into* the paintings," she admitted.

"Are you saying you're a witch?"

Rico's disbelieving laugh set her teeth on edge. He really had tried to negate Pueblo beliefs in his mind. Charlotte wanted to whomp him like she used to as a girl when he would tease her mercilessly. But they weren't kids anymore. They weren't even friends. Since she'd returned to New Mexico, their relationship had been strictly professional. He'd hung a few of her paintings and had promised that if she stayed long enough to produce enough pieces, Milagro Gallery would sponsor a show featuring her work.

"I returned to Sena Pueblo to connect with our people, our culture, our history," she said, wishing he felt the same way. "I want to know everything there is to know."

"Including witchcraft," he said, suddenly turning serious.

"What my grandmother teaches me is not evil. It's a form of meditation. An inner journey. A dream state. I don't know how this happened. One minute I was staring at Joe's painting and grieving for the loss of a talented artist, the next minute I felt my mind drift to the desert area he'd painted. I didn't know what to think. It was as if I was pulled there by some higher power. Rico, I truly believe Joe's paintings hold the clues to his and Sanchez's murders. Maybe to the human remains they found there, too."

But Rico didn't look convinced. He didn't even look open to the possibility.

"That's what I thought," Charlotte muttered, trying to cover her disappointment in him. "You don't hold the old beliefs."

"I can't say that I do."

"Then you wouldn't understand." Rico wasn't someone she could talk to about this, after all. "I guess the only thing Pueblo you want to know about is how much money you can make on our art."

His features stiffened into a cold mask. "That's not fair."

"Neither is murder."

With that, Charlotte swept away from him to the front door, unlocked it, and left the gallery.

RICO STARED after her.

He felt her disdain for him. It shouldn't make him uncomfortable, but it did.

Turning to Joe's painting, he wondered what Charlotte had seen in it. Then he shook his head, chased away the fanciful idea that she might actually have been able to enter the painted landscape to search for clues. Delores Reyna had certainly influenced her granddaughter to take up the old ways.

Once he'd believed in them, too, but no more. He was no longer an impressionable boy who believed in magic.

Now he was a businessman, and a successful one at that. He didn't have time for superstitious nonsense. As a matter of fact, he had work to do, uncrating some new sculptures.

Rico locked the gallery door, but before getting back to work, looked for Charlotte through the display window. She was across the street unlocking her red SUV, probably the nicest, newest vehicle on the pueblo. As if she could feel him watching her, she glanced back toward the gallery and, for a moment, he felt as if their gazes connected, as if she were probing him for any sign of the Rico she knew.

Charlotte's looks might have matured, but he would have known her anywhere. She'd inherited the best of both her worlds—her magnetic dark eyes, her thick fall of black hair and her sun-kissed skin from her Indian father—her height, her slender, elegant figure and her fine features from her Anglo mother. She'd met the promise of her girlhood, when he'd been secretly smitten with her.

Not that he'd ever told her. Or anyone. Good thing, because at ten, she'd been dragged kicking and screaming out East—and out of his life forever.

Or so he'd thought.

But now she was back in New Mexico and every time they were together, something sparked between them.

Or maybe it was just that they had different value systems and she scorned his.

A sense of longing filled him as Charlotte broke the connection and slipped into her vehicle and drove off as fast as she could. Was she that disgusted with him? Or did she fear wanting something out of her control?

Rico flicked off all but the display window lights, then headed back for the storeroom where he got to the new crates filled with artwork that had come in that afternoon.

What was so wrong with his values anyway? He ran a thriving business that gave Native American artists a shot at making money and maybe even a name for themselves. So what if his profits had allowed him to buy a *casita* in the right part of town? No way did he ever want to live on Sena Pueblo again, and he didn't see what attraction it held for someone like Charlotte Reyna.

Would he seem more noble to her if he emulated his parents and siblings? His mother and two sisters sold souvenirs in tourist shops. His father and three brothers worked on the construction of fake adobe buildings—when there *was* work. He'd done that for a while as a teenager before he'd pursued an education so that he could work at something that would get him as far away from poverty as possible. While studying for a business degree, he'd gotten a job in a gallery where he had learned everything he could about art. Later, he'd been given the seed money to open his own gallery from a wealthy Anglo art patron who'd also happened to be his lover.

Surely, Charlotte would look down on him for that.

No sense in his thinking about her. They were worlds apart in everything but their love for art. He should put her right out of his mind.

But as he tried to do so, Rico knew he couldn't. Charlotte seemed to be set on putting herself in the middle of a mess that could get her killed. He couldn't let that happened.

No matter what she thought about him, he would protect her always.

Or at least until she returned to New York where she belonged.

Chapter Two

Rico's image stayed with Charlotte longer than she liked. The gallery owner bothered her, kept her slightly off her game whenever in his presence.

So Charlotte was relieved when she arrived back on Sena Pueblo and parked in front of the tiny adobe house she now called home. Pulling stray hairs back from her face, she brushed her ear and realized her earring was gone. It must have slipped out of her ear and she hadn't noticed. The earrings weren't expensive, but she'd really liked the Southwestern stylized coyotes she'd bought at a little jewelry shop on a side street in Santa Fe. She checked herself and the floor of her vehicle. Nothing. Then she remembered thinking she'd heard something hit the ground back at the gallery. That had to be it.

Hoping she would find the missing earring at the gallery the next day, Charlotte removed its mate and slipped it into her pocket. Then she left the vehicle and headed for the house. She loved living with Delores Reyna, her late father's mother. The moment she stepped inside, her stomach growled at her. She could smell onion and garlic and pork cooking together on the stove. She knew that her grandmother was making *posole,* a traditional spicy corn and pork stew, a dish meant to celebrate life's blessings.

Charlotte recognized her many blessings despite the terrible situation with Joe's death and her own strange involvement. She crossed the red-tiled floor through the living area with its whitewashed walls decorated with Indian art, including two of her own landscapes— one hung on either side of the corner kiva fireplace. In the kitchen, dried spices hung in bunches over a tiled food preparation table, Grandmother's base of operation. Dressed in her typical calf-length denim skirt, plain white blouse and necklace of tiny turquoise animals, her silver hair plaited in twin braids that hung down her back to her waist, she was turning a bowl of boiled chilies and water into a paste.

Charlotte hugged the short, well-rounded woman and kissed her wrinkled cheek. "That smells…yummy. What can I do to help?"

"You can get the bowl of corn and add the contents to the pot."

Grandmother prepared *posole* corn the old way rather than buying canned hominy, which she insisted wasn't as good. She'd already put hard kernels of field corn to soak in powdered lime and water for several hours. The corn kernels had swollen and the liquid had already evaporated. So Charlotte did as instructed, using a wooden spoon to mix the corn into the cooking meat and broth, wondering if she would ever learn to make the traditional meals that were, in her opinion, an art form.

Then Grandmother added the chilies. "It needs to cook another fifteen minutes or so. You rest and I'll call you when it's ready."

Thinking it was her grandmother who should be doing the resting—her eyes were shadowed with dark smudges and she didn't have quite as much spring to her step—Charlotte refrained from saying anything lest she hurt the elderly woman's feelings. "How about I set the table instead?"

Besides, she would rather stay busy than give Rico another opening to get to her. Unless she kept herself distracted, thoughts of the man consumed her. Not that they should. They had much in common…and yet so little. She shook her head and gathered bowls and spoons for the table.

How excited she had been returning to New Mexico. To the heritage that called to her very soul. The heritage Rico personally rejected.

Rico called her work genius. She guessed that would be proven or not when she had enough for a show of her own. She'd adapted her painting style to the rugged beauty of this native land, had made landscapes more interesting by incorporating stylized figures representing the people. She was on the brink of something she hadn't even anticipated when she'd made the decision to head to the Southwest.

Charlotte hadn't anticipated her connection to Joe's paintings, either, to this power that had unwrapped itself and presented itself to her like a gift. Since she'd arrived at the pueblo, Grandmother had been teaching her about the spiritual energy of being a Native American. The elderly woman had counseled her, taught her to seek her totem and to use meditation to journey to a spiritual level.

But now Charlotte had gone a step further and she didn't even know how. She was seeing things that weren't real…and that somehow were…

If only she could talk to Rico about it. But of course she couldn't. He would simply laugh at her again. His earlier amusement at her expense still stung.

"What is wrong, Granddaughter?"

Blinking, Charlotte started. She realized she was standing frozen at the table in front of a bowl, spoon in hand. She set down the utensil and shrugged far more casually than she was feeling. "Oh, I was just thinking."

"About something serious, it seems."

"Rico."

Part of the truth. While she'd mentioned her connection to the paintings—and Grandmother had warned her to watch for a black witch at work—Charlotte didn't want to worry the elderly woman with the danger she'd felt in her latest journey.

Grandmother smiled. "I remember thinking when you and Rico were still children that you would make a fine couple."

"We're adults now."

"Yes, and now it is time for you to recognize your destiny. You will make beautiful children together."

A thrill shot through Charlotte at the thought, yet she shook her head. "My destiny doesn't include Rico. He doesn't approve of me, of the things you teach me."

"Rico had a difficult time as a young man. He didn't know where he fit in this mixed land of ours. His Spanish grandfather, who owns a big-deal ranch near Taos, wouldn't even recognize him because Rico's mother had gone below her station when she'd married a man from the pueblo."

"How horrible," Charlotte murmured, her brow furrowing. She'd never heard that before.

Her Anglo mother's relatives had been a bit reserved

until they'd gotten to know her, but at least when her
mother had taken her back East, no one had turned her
away. And when she'd left to come home to New Mexico, her mother's mother had cried and had assured
Charlotte she would always be welcomed back to the
Upchurch family home if she changed her mind.

"At least Rico has two parents and siblings who love
him," Charlotte said.

"Yes. But his parents were too busy trying to put
food on the table for their big family to see to Rico's spiritual needs. He had no one in his life to guide him."

"And now it's too late."

"No. It is never too late to become enlightened."
Grandmother's eyes sparkled and a knowing smile curved
her lips. "Perhaps that is part of your destiny, also."

RICO ENTERED the Bucking Bronc Bar and immediately
spotted Tom and Luke at a spot in back near the pool
table. He ordered a beer from the bartender and then
made his way through the crowd.

Bucking Bronc used to be a local place, but few
places really remained for the locals in Santa Fe. Tourists everywhere. You could spot the ones with "turquoise poisoning" a mile away. They were all duded up
in hats and boots and lots and lots of Indian jewelry.
Their eyes followed you, hungry and envious, as if they
wanted to come up to you and ask what it was like to
be in your skin.

That was the part he hated most…and the part most
useful in his making a good living.

"Anything new?" he asked his friends as he claimed
the empty chair they'd left for him.

Tom quickly told him about the attack on Jessie. "I

made sure she got checked out. She had to report in after, of course."

"How is she?" Rico asked. "And what are you doing here?"

"She's okay, though she's down at the mouth about having to back off the case. She's still doing some kind of paperwork. She said she'd call when she was done."

Rico felt hollow inside. Just seeing Tom and Jessie together the past couple of days told him all he needed to know about their loving relationship. And that, after Luke and Ashley had hit it off. Both men were sure to be walking down an aisle sometime soon.

Looked like he was the odd man out. Permanently.

For a moment Rico saw Charlotte in his mind's eye, all beautiful and intense and wrapped up in Joe's painting. Then she faced him and her expression was exactly as it had been before she'd left the gallery earlier.

Rico clenched his jaw and cleared his mind. No sense in thinking of her.

"So, did Gonzales beat his butt to the cabin to investigate?" he asked Tom.

"Yeah, he got there. Didn't find anything to break the case."

Luke said, "Sounds like our criminal is someone close to the gallery. I mean, the janitor was involved. Then Joe's paintings were stolen. And now they're burned. So the guy's bound to have a gallery connection."

"Maybe," Tom said.

Rico thought his friend was holding something back. As to Luke's intimation that the killer might be associated with the gallery…employee Jay Soto came to mind. The kid sometimes had his nose where it didn't belong, but to Rico's knowledge, he didn't have a motive. Now if the murder had happened *after* the theft, he might think that Jay had gotten a little greedy and that Joe had figured it out and had been eliminated.

Cutting into Rico's thoughts, Luke mused, "Or maybe the casino manager is our villain. He seems to have a thing for Joe's paintings."

"More likely he has a thing for Jessie's mom." Tom took a long swallow of beer. "He helped her out of a jam twice that we know of by buying Joe's paintings from her."

"Probably at half the value. Don't worry, he'll make a profit." Rico frowned at his buddy as Tom tapped his fingers against the beer mug. He was getting a peculiar feeling that Tom had a theory of his own. "Okay, what is it you're *not* saying?"

"Look, Rico, I don't like this."

"None of us do," Luke said. "If you know something, tell us."

Tom cursed and then spat out, "Paxton Gardner. It was his place where the paintings were burned. Jessie thinks he might have had something to do with Joe's murder. But, damn, if he tried to kill his own daughter…"

"He'd be the biggest bastard going." And Tom might know things about Gardner that he couldn't talk about since he was the man's lawyer, Rico thought.

"Right now the most important thing for me is keeping Ashley safe," Luke stated. "I'm going to get her out of here, away from the murderer. Now that I've found the woman I want to share the rest of my life with, I don't intend to let anything happen to her, so I'm taking her to her parents'. I might as well get the meet-and-greet over with."

Rico figured Luke was worried about the Donaldsons' reaction to him not because he was Pueblo Indian—Ashley herself being of mixed heritage—but because he'd been in jail.

"Ashley loves you enough that she'll make her parents see what a catch you are," Rico said. "And even if they don't see it, she'll stand by you, so no need to worry."

"Who the hell is worrying?" Luke asked gruffly. "Not me."

It was a lie and they all knew it. But rather than give their friend a hard time, Rico and Tom toasted Luke and wished him Godspeed.

And then Rico was on his way home. Alone. Wishing he weren't.

What was wrong with him? He could have a different woman every night of the week if he wanted. Only he didn't want that. What he did want he couldn't have, so he might as well get over it and concentrate on the gallery. He had a new shipment coming in from an artist based in Taos, so he tried to concentrate on that… but in his mind, those portraits of old Taos hippies with the llamas they raised faded, leaving one stunning face in their stead.

Charlotte.

Once more he was watching her as she sat in front of Joe Cordova's painting and grew more and more intense only to seem as if she'd left her body and gone somewhere else. Not that he believed in that stuff, but what if…

Rico's heart hammered in his chest as he realized Charlotte could get herself into big, big trouble.

HE FINGERED the silver coyote. How ironic that his favorite totem had found its way to him and confirmed what he'd suspected for days.

Charlotte Reyna was trouble.

He'd finally caught the woman snooping around where she didn't belong. The coyote substantiated her identity. He couldn't help being freaked out, though, wondering how it was that he'd run into her on one of his journeys. Where had she gotten the know-how?

Delores Reyna. Of course.

The old busybody must be instructing her granddaughter in the old ways. Not that she would have the energy to do that for much longer. Besides, Charlotte hadn't been back in Santa Fe long enough to learn what she had to do.

Not unless…

He didn't want to think about the innate power she might possess. He preferred to think of her stumbling into his journey by mistake. Or by sheer luck. He'd found the earring in front of Joe Cordova's painting, though. A painting whose landscape he haunted.

How had he missed this one when he'd stolen the others? He cursed the fact that he'd had no opportunity to remove it—the damn thing was still hanging in the gallery and now Tafoya had tightened security.

What was the connection between the painting and the earlier intrusion? It almost seemed as if the painting itself was a portal of some kind.

The idea made his rage surface.

Charlotte Reyna could spell disaster if she was allowed to continue unchecked. The old woman wouldn't stand a chance against him. But Charlotte?

He stared down at the earring in his palm, still warm with her energy, and he thought of how to use it to put a stop to her snooping for once and for all.

Chapter Three

"What is it you think you see?" Rico asked, breaking into Charlotte's thoughts, wherever they might have wandered.

Standing in front of Joe's painting once more, Charlotte started and turned troubled eyes to him. "You wouldn't want to know."

"Try me."

She moved away from the painting and from him and ducked her head so that her dark hair veiled her face. He loved seeing her hair loose, imagined the silky feel of it waterfalling through his hands. She was especially stunning today in embroidered low-rise jeans, a thin suede halter top trimmed with turquoise, coral and feathers, and leather bracelets to match. More and more, she'd been playing up her Indian heritage in every way. It suited her.

"Charlotte, please. You worry me."

Her head snapped toward him and her eyes suddenly looked too big for her delicately featured face. She couldn't hide her surprise.

"Worrying about someone means you care," she said softly.

Rico's pulse jumped, but he forced himself to lean casually against a pillar. "Of course I care about the next new artist who is going to make a name for herself in my gallery."

"Is that all?"

His pulse ticked in his throat. For a moment he wanted to tell her no. He wanted to tell her the truth. He wanted to tell her that she filled his waking moments and his dreams.

Instead he said, "Of course I would care if something bad happened to anyone I knew."

And he caught a shimmer of disappointment before she closed herself off from him.

"Try me," he said again.

"I'm assuming you recognize the canyon."

"I'm familiar with it," he said, eyes sweeping to the vein of orange rock in the wall.

Fingers trembling, Charlotte touched the arroyo cutting into the *bajada* at the base of the cliff. "The fine white lines that look like sun-bleached juniper—"

"The skeleton."

She nodded.

"You told Tom that you were simply looking for another meaning Joe gave the canvas. But yesterday you told *me* you were taking some kind of a journey."

He held his breath, waiting. She appeared uncomfortable and she was absently tugging at her left earlobe.

"Both are true. When I first began studying Joe's paintings, it was with the eye of another artist eager to learn. But something about his canvases pulled at me, and I found I was seeing things…signs. And as I told you yesterday, to my surprise, I was suddenly in the painting, crossing the landscape not with my eyes but with my feet. Somehow I imagine walking through what I see on the canvas…then things around me change… shift…and suddenly I'm someplace else…"

Her voice faded and she seemed distracted. She shook her head and frowned as if she were uneasy about something.

She'd been right—he didn't like this. "You always had an active imagination. You need to concentrate on reality."

"I can't control it, Rico." She was pacing in front of the painting now, her gaze glued to it again. "It's as though Joe were reaching out from the grave asking me to find his killer."

"Don't be stupid!"

Charlotte gasped and stepped back. About to apologize, to say that he meant she should leave it to the tribal police and keep herself safe, Rico thought better of it. Maybe being frank with her would keep her from going off the deep end.

"I feel sorry for you, Rico Tafoya. You don't believe in anything or anyone. I'm sure you could do without knowing who killed Joe as long as your business didn't suffer. Money is the only thing you care about!"

Rico clenched his jaw. She was wrong, but he wasn't going to argue with her. Let her think the worst of him. He just didn't want her to get hurt or worse.

"Why is it you're here today?" he asked, hoping to distract her from the murders. "Did you bring in new paintings?"

"No. I lost an earring yesterday," she said, voice stiff. Her fingers went to her lobe again. "I was looking for it. A silver coyote?"

"Haven't seen it."

Charlotte's eyes shifted past him. "Jay, you didn't find an earring around here, did you?"

"Sorry."

Turning to see his assistant standing in the doorway, Rico wondered how long Jay had been there and how much of their conversation he'd overheard.

"Then I'd better get going," Charlotte said.

Rico turned back to see that she was staring at the painting again. "Where?" he asked.

Charlotte gave herself a shake. "To work, of course."

But Rico didn't believe she meant home to paint. She was acting too oddly. He'd bet she was going to go into the desert to find some clue to Joe's murder. He thought to stop her but knew he couldn't. He would only make her angrier. So instead, he would follow her.

He waited until she was out of the gallery before telling Jay to take over for him.

Charlotte was parked on the street. He slipped out the back way into the small side lot and slid into his truck. Luckily it was black like so many other vehicles in the area. Hopefully she wouldn't notice him following her as she headed out of town.

That she turned down a dirt road a half mile before the entrance to the pueblo didn't surprise him. Rico slowed, meaning to put more distance between them. The vehicle would raise dust and if she looked back, he didn't want her to spot him. He wanted to see for himself what she was up to.

There was only one place to go on this road. She was heading out for the wilderness area where Joe had done his landscapes.

Where a skeleton had been found.

Not all that far from where Joe had been murdered.

What the hell did she think she was up to? Letting her imagination run wild while meditating in front of a painting was one thing. But going to the scene of the crime—crimes rather, albeit decades apart—was another.

She could get herself killed….

CHARLOTTE'S HEART BEAT faster as she approached the area where Joe had been killed. The "road" couldn't be more primitive—simply a rough cut in the earth to clear the path for crime scene vehicles. Luckily she had four-wheel drive and could go practically anywhere.

Why here, though?

She knew coming to the murder scene could be dangerous…and yet she couldn't help herself. All morning, even before she had gone into the gallery, Joe's landscapes had called to her, an unspoken whisper in her mind. With each hour the urge had grown stronger, had filled her thoughts until she could think of nothing else, almost as if some unknown magic had her in its grip.

Of course she was doing this to herself. She had to be. Just as she had somehow been thrusting herself into Joe's paintings. It was all tied together, she was certain. She'd found clues through the paintings. What would she find in person?

The scrub of high desert turned into rock and she entered the mouth of the canyon. Leaving her vehicle, she stared in awe. This was the first time she'd seen the setting that Joe had painted so many times in person.

Slowly she turned, taking it all in—the dry arroyo, a huge tumble of boulders, what looked to be a cave tucked high along a ledge in the cliffs.

Focused on the cave opening, Charlotte felt the urge

to check it out. The cave called to her, the sensation taking on a life of its own.

She felt the urge rush through her blood, heard wind rushing through the cave, calling her name.

Eyes fixed on the ledge, she began to move forward, placing one foot in front of the other, slowly at first, then faster as her heart sped up. Soon she was jogging, her boots pounding against the loose earth, surrounding her with a fine cloud of dust.

Then suddenly flapping wings rushed past, startling her, making her clumsy. More wings had her turning, searching for the bird that wasn't there until her feet tangled one around the other and she stumbled hard into a patch of brush.

Brush that gave way...

Charlotte started and gave a shout as the earth crumbled beneath her feet. She reached out to snatch at a clump of desert grass, but it came free in her hand. Her stomach somersaulted as she fell...fell...fell...

Landing with a thud, she dropped sideways and caught herself from landing on her face with her hands.

Shaken, she took a steadying breath and stood upright. The opening was several feet above her. She was caught in some kind of a trap.

Unhurt, she looked for a way out, but the walls were smooth and offered her hands and feet no purchase.

She closed her eyes and cursed. She was going to have to call someone to get her out of here. And there was only one person who came to mind.

Rico.

She pulled out her cell.

Only one problem. No signal.

Now what?

If she had a stick, she could use it as a makeshift tool to dig little notches for her hands and feet and climb out. *If* the earth didn't immediately crumble and collapse under her weight. Of course she had nothing with her but the stupid cell phone.

Charlotte was considering turning the useless phone into a minishovel when footsteps slid fear along her spine. Her heart hammered and the sound of blood rushing through her head was so loud she thought whoever was up there could hear her.

She had no weapon.

She was defenseless.

Was she the next to die?

Chapter Four

One minute Charlotte was there, the next she was gone, and Rico had only looked away for a few seconds. His heart kick-started. Cursing, feeling his pulse respond, he quickly navigated the desert floor in the direction he'd last seen her. How the hell had she disappeared so fast?

A dry wind picked up sandy dust from an area directly in front of him. He slowed and protected his eyes until it settled. When he looked again, he saw it—a maw in the earth that hadn't been there before. He made straight for it, knelt at the opening and peered in.

Despite the shift from sun to shadow, he caught movement and automatically called, "Charlotte?"

"Rico?" She made a sound of relief. "You scared the life out of me."

"Back at you," he muttered, reaching in. "Take my hand."

His eyes quickly adjusted. He could see her dust-covered form now. She stretched upward awkwardly, as though she were stiff or hurting. Her fingers reached for his but the tips barely brushed together.

"That's not going to work." Concern growing, Rico flattened himself against the earth. "Try now."

Her hand slid against his, and although he closed his over hers, he couldn't get the leverage needed to lift her out of the hole. Reluctantly he let go.

"Hang on. I'll find something I can use."

Nothing that would prove helpful lay in the area around the trap. An animal trap, one big enough to contain a mountain lion or a bear…

Moving away from the maw, he looked around. No water here. No food. Nothing that he could see to lure an animal this way. And if it had been here when Tom and Jessie found the skeleton, surely Tom would have noticed and told him.

Or maybe the trap wasn't meant for a wild animal…

He could hardly believe it, but it seemed that someone was hunting human game.

Spotting a small juniper tree, Rico hurried over to it. He reached into the side of his right boot and removed a knife. A weapon didn't go with his present persona as a successful gallery owner, but it did go with his past. Having the knife on him at all times gave him a sense of security he needed, even after all these years.

Good thing he had it now. It made wresting a thick, six-foot branch from the stout tree a hell of a lot easier. He leaned the branch against a V in the tree and tested it with his weight. When it held, he figured it would do.

"Got something!" he yelled to Charlotte, hoping to ease her anxiety even as he took another look around for signs of human life.

The trap had been dug *after* Joe had been murdered, *after* the skeleton had been found. Which meant the murderer suspected someone would be snooping around.

Now the question was, had the murderer known that someone would be Charlotte?

Rico told himself that he was being ridiculous.

How would the murderer have known that Charlotte would come out here looking for clues?

Dragging the branch back to the opening, Rico said, "I'll have you out of there in a minute."

"Good. It can't be too soon for me."

The relief in Charlotte's voice made Rico take another intense look around before putting himself in a vulnerable position. As far as he could tell, they were completely alone. He got to his knees and peered in at Charlotte, whose nerves were showing in the rapid way she was rubbing her arm.

"Take this branch and lean it up against the side of the trap, then use it to lever yourself up as high as you can go," he said, lowering it to her.

Charlotte did as he instructed, then climbed onto the branch and started crawling upward. She was stronger and more athletic than she looked. When she got almost to the top, she started to stand. A warning crack made Rico reach down for her.

"Hand!" he ordered.

One hand plunged upward, out through the opening. He grabbed onto the leather bracelet, which gave him a better grip, and pulled until the other hand shot out. No sooner did he have hold of both and started to pull her out when another crack slid up his spine. Suddenly he had all Charlotte's weight tugging at him. In a panic that she would be hurt if he let go, he threw himself backward and somehow managed to pull her halfway out of the hole.

Charlotte flailed for a bit, then suddenly shot forward and landed on top of him. Though the air was knocked out of him, Rico snapped his arms around her back and held her tight. They were both winded, gasping for air. Even so, the intimacy of the situation quickly aroused him.

The last thing he wanted was to let her go.

He could tell she knew it, too. Her eyelids lowered and she licked her lips. No struggle, no attempt to free herself. They were still breathing heavy, no longer from exertion, but from the possibility…

And then Charlotte pushed at his chest. "You can let me up now."

Rico couldn't help himself. He waited a moment before he complied and savored every nuance of her body as she slid off him. Then she was on her feet, quick as a jackrabbit. Following suit, he slipped an arm around her waist.

"Hey," she protested.

He swung her around, away from the maw. "I just didn't want to have to do that again."

"Oh."

Waiting only until she caught her breath, Rico asked, "Now what the hell do you think you can do out here?"

Charlotte gave him a mutinous expression. "I just wanted to see the place for myself."

"So you could solve Joe's murder?"

"I don't know. Maybe."

"How?"

Charlotte flushed. "After what happened with the painting…"

"You thought you could do a repeat performance out here?" Not that he believed it.

"Yes, why not? What if I found a clue—"

"What if you found the murderer?" he countered, his gaze covering the landscape. "What then?"

"I didn't think that far ahead."

"Obviously not. You acted before you thought and look where it got you."

"So I ran into an animal trap."

"Maybe that trap was meant for *you*, Charlotte." Though he still didn't know how that could be.

She gaped at him and her eyes widened, and he hated that he put fear in them. But she *needed* to be afraid, he told himself. She *needed* to know that she couldn't run off on her own to catch a murderer and not suffer consequences.

Rico fought the instinct to take her into his arms and hold her close. He was certain she wouldn't appreciate the gesture at this moment.

If ever.

"I'm assuming nothing is broken," he said gruffly.

"Just bruised."

"Good, let's get out of here."

He thought she might argue with him, but fear trumped stubbornness. She swung past him and headed back toward her SUV. She was limping. He clenched his jaw and set after her, all the while keeping alert for any further danger. It wasn't until they were back to the parked vehicles that Charlotte seemed to realize what a mess she was.

"Great, just great," she said, swatting at her jeans. "My clothes are filthy."

"You should see your face and hair."

"The last thing Grandmother needs is to worry about me."

"Then don't worry her. Come back into town. You can clean up at my place."

CHARLOTTE TOLD HERSELF she'd agreed to go with Rico for Grandmother's sake, but as she pulled up in front of his *casita* immediately behind him, she admitted she was equally curious to see how he lived.

Quite well, she decided.

Hidden behind a coyote fence, the 1920s Pueblo-style *casa* was graced with a portal that swept along the front of the building. And beneath the porch roof was a hand-carved wooden bench and a couple of cane-and-cushioned chairs. A small patio to the side held a gas grill that was state of the art.

The inside was equally inviting with Mission-style furniture, punched-tin light fixtures and pale gold walls laden with Southwestern art, no doubt from Milagro Gallery. A home theater was set up in the living room—a sage-green sectional sat in front of a giant LCD placed in a carved, green-and-white-washed *trastero* that took up a quarter of the wall. A peek at the open kitchen revealed counters of Talavera tile.

Remembering the tough kid Rico had been on the pueblo, the one whose room had held only a bed and a beat-up stereo, she murmured, "Wow, this isn't like the Rico I remember at all."

"Because I'm not that Rico anymore," he reminded her, his voice sharp.

Part of her wanted to say too bad. But that would be unfair of her. He'd done well for himself and why shouldn't he want to show off his success. His not believing in the old ways anymore, his using his Indian heritage to his advantage…that didn't make him a bad person, she told herself. Just one who didn't have much in common with her anymore.

"This way."

Rico led her through the bedroom. Charlotte was sure the place had another bath, so why was he taking her to the one in his personal space? She avoided staring at the four-poster draped in sage-colored bedding, but the mere thought of being in that bed, the fireplace in the corner warming the room with firelight, set her pulse humming.

He stood just outside the bathroom doorway, so that she felt his heat as she slid past.

"I hope you don't plan on standing guard," she muttered. "There's no danger here." Unless from him.

"A shower sounds pretty good to me, too."

Did he assume because he'd saved her she would shower—and do other things—with him?

Charlotte was about to say something sharp when she realized that Rico was teasing her. His eyes had a light in them that was familiar and warm. A light she hadn't noticed since returning to New Mexico. A light that made her uncertain about everything she thought she knew about him.

"The shower tower has jets that'll help keep you from tightening up. Enjoy yourself," he said as he swung the door shut.

The bath was as beautiful as the rest of the house. Stunning art tiles, some with hand-painted horses. She stripped and turned on the water and cursed Rico under her breath. He'd planted thoughts in her mind that she couldn't avoid. The shower wasn't quite as relaxing as it was meant to be.

When she left the bathroom, it was to hear the strains of a native flute. She followed the pleasant sound into the living area where Rico was pouring coffee into a couple of mugs. He'd showered, too, and his feet were bare, his hair wet and loose and as long as hers.

Something primal stirred in her belly. She couldn't stop looking at him. Wishing. Remembering.

His brow furrowed. "What?" He handed her a mug of coffee.

"I just had an image of the tough kid you used to be."

"I was an even tougher teenager," he admitted. "Luke and Tom and I ran wild. We used to make bets on who could be the baddest…"

Which Charlotte was pretty sure would be Rico.

"…and then Luke was railroaded into jail for a crime he didn't commit. That's when I realized that being even part Indian could be a liability and that I needed to find a way out of the pueblo for good."

Even though the confession made Charlotte understand the way Rico thought a bit better, she said, "You can't really turn your back on your roots. I'm a perfect example of someone who was given a whole new life, but I found I couldn't just ignore the old one."

"That won't happen to me."

Rico's assertion disappointed Charlotte. She reminded herself of what her grandmother had told her. That Rico's own Spanish grandfather with the big ranch near Taos had never recognized him. That had to be a sore spot still.

"A dollar for your thoughts, Charlotte."

She blinked and brought him into focus. "You mean, a penny."

"Inflation." He grinned at her.

"I was just wondering if you were truly happy."

His grin faded and his voice stiffened. "Why wouldn't I be? I have everything a man could want now."

A statement that unsettled Charlotte. Finishing her coffee, she thanked him for the rescue and made her excuses. "I need to get back to the pueblo."

Now Rico's visage darkened. "You'll be vulnerable

there. You can stay here for a couple of days until the murderer is caught."

Stay with Rico? A flush shot through her. She wished she could deny any attraction to him, but it was useless. Charlotte didn't know which would be more dangerous—putting herself in the murderer's line of fire…or Rico's.

"Thanks for the offer," she said, getting up to leave, hoping he didn't notice her sudden case of nerves. "I'll be fine."

On the drive back to the pueblo, Rico filled her thoughts and Charlotte wondered why the idea of being close to him scared her so. As a kid, she'd had a crush on him. When she was with him now, however, she recognized an emptiness in him that he would never admit to. An emptiness that kept her from wanting to get closer. Rico needed to respect himself enough to blend the new ways with the old. Until he did, she would simply have to accept him as a friend, nothing more.

A friend good enough to be concerned about her, to watch her back, to want to protect her. A reassuring thought in case she really was in danger.

Chapter Five

Charlotte approached the gallery later that afternoon with a sense of trepidation. She'd barely begun working on a new painting when Rico had called her and asked her to come back to Santa Fe. He'd said it was important, and she'd heard an urgency in his voice. She assumed he'd learned something about the murder.

Her stomach fluttered as she opened the door and walked into the soothing atmosphere of the gallery. A CD was playing and a smudge stick burning. Other than Jay Soto and two women looking over the cases of pawn, the place was near deserted.

She caught Jay's attention. "Rico?"

"In back. He's unpacking some canvases."

Feeling Jay's eyes following her, Charlotte let herself into the back room. Rico was bent over a table, removing the packaging from a large canvas. He was in his gallery owner disguise. Thankfully. She was more comfortable with this Rico than the one she'd seen in his home, where he'd gotten to her more than she'd liked.

She cleared her throat to let him know she was here.

Rico turned to face her and her stomach fluttered. Maybe she wasn't comfortable with *any* Rico.

"Is there a break in the case?" she asked.

"Not exactly. I asked you to come for a couple of reasons." He walked over to the desk and fetched an envelope.

"The check for your painting cleared, so I thought you would like to be paid."

Carefully avoiding his fingers, Charlotte took the envelope from him. Getting some significant money for her work should be more of a thrill. She was too distracted to do more than put it in her pocket.

"Aren't you even going to make sure the amount is correct?"

"I trust you."

"Do you?"

Charlotte realized she did. For all that he had morphed on the outside, she thought his intrinsic honesty and loyalty hadn't changed.

"So what's the other thing you wanted to see me about?" she asked, hearing footsteps behind her.

Charlotte turned as Tom Lahi entered the storeroom. So part of why she was here *did* have to do with the murder. Tom was looking tense and clutching a large envelope. Greetings were brief and Tom got right to the point.

"You know Jessie was attacked on her father's land, right?" he asked. "Did Rico tell you about Joe's canvases being burned?"

"No, Rico must have forgotten to tell me," Charlotte said, wondering why he hadn't. "What a loss."

"Everything was destroyed but this."

Tom fumbled with the large, sealed plastic bag. From it, he took a folder. Inside lay a piece of painted canvas, its edges charred. The broad strokes of rich browns and oranges and greens were familiar—the canyon in the desert. An area not far from where she'd been attacked.

"Jessie and I talked about this," Tom said. "She already dusted for fingerprints, but nothing. We agreed that you needed to see it. She signed it out of evidence, so she could take it to an expert to have it analyzed. You're that expert."

"Me? But forensics—"

"I trust you more, Charlotte. I know you said you figured out those clues through interpretation, but after the stuff that's been going on, I'm open to believing it was more. Some kind of psychic thing. I hope you'll agree to help. I fear that if we don't get to the truth, the authorities will railroad another Indian and give an Anglo a pass."

"You don't mean Jessie's dad?"

"Unfortunately. Paxton Gardner has to be involved somehow. The land where the canvases burned belongs to him. And right now, if anyone is investigating him, we don't know about it. Jessie took herself out of the loop after she was attacked."

Charlotte whipped her gaze to Rico. He hadn't told her that, either. Someone had attacked Jessie…the same person who'd set a trap that *she* had fallen into?

She nodded at Tom. "I see why you're worried."

"People with money can buy their way out of anything," Rico said.

A statement that was a little extreme, Charlotte thought. Her east coast relatives had money, but they also had integrity. Still, it wasn't looking good for Gardner.

Taking the folder from Tom, Charlotte touched the remains of Joe's painting. Her fingertips immediately grew hot, as if the canvas were burning them. She snatched her hand away, certain the shard held important secrets if only she was brave enough to explore them.

"How long can I keep this?" she asked Tom.

"I was hoping you could just see what you could see now and give me the scoop."

"It doesn't work that way." She couldn't perform on command. Not that Tom knew about her out-of-body experiences. He probably thought she could simply interpret what she saw and give him a clue as she had before. "I—I need some time to study it."

"I hate to say this is a rush job, but the sooner, the better."

"I'll see what I can do. At least give me until the morning."

Tom didn't seem terribly happy with that, but he nodded in agreement. "We appreciate your help."

"Tell Jessie I'll do my best…and that I hope to heaven her father isn't involved in this, after all."

Rico wasn't saying anything, but his jaw had hardened and he had the look of a man straining for action. In the seconds it took Tom to take his leave, Rico's expression shifted to neutral, yet his body language told another story.

Before Charlotte could question him, he said, "Why don't you go to my place instead of the pueblo? No one would think to find you there."

Charlotte wanted to ask, *Like whom?* but she caught his drift. He meant the murderer, of course.

"Thanks, but I need to check on Grandmother. She was very tired today and was sleeping when I left. She never naps, so I want to make sure she's all right."

The truth if not the reason she didn't want to bunk

with Rico. His jaw tightened but, to Charlotte's relief, he didn't argue with her.

As a concession she said, "I'll call you immediately if I see or feel anything in the canvas."

"Maybe I should come to the pueblo with you. You shouldn't be alone."

"I won't be. Grandmother will be there."

She left unspoken—*Someone who believes in Pueblo magic.* Rico would only make her nervous. It would be impossible to let down her barriers with him looking over her shoulder.

Thankfully, Rico got her drift and let it drop.

RICO WAITED mere seconds after Charlotte left the office to follow her into the gallery. A furtive movement in his peripheral vision stopped him cold. He turned to see his assistant ducking back from the area.

"Jay!"

Jay Soto stopped in his tracks. "Something you need, boss?"

"For you to mind your own business. I'm tired of catching you listening in to what doesn't concern you. Are we clear on this?"

"Yeah, sure," Jay said tersely.

"If you know something about Joe's murder," Rico said, "spit it out."

"Me? What the hell would I know?"

Realizing a couple of tourists had just entered the gallery, Rico inclined his head. "Then go justify your salary."

By the time Jay approached the two women, he was wearing a very different face, one far more appealing, and his chambray shirt was open just enough to show

his smooth chest. How many faces did he have? Rico
wondered, leaving the gallery and getting into his truck.

By the time he hit the street, Charlotte was long gone,
of course. Not that he'd meant to follow her this time.
With her concern over her grandmother, he was certain
she really would head for home.

While he was heading out to find Paxton Gardner.

Still, Rico couldn't help but think about Charlotte as
he drove. Would she really be able to read something
off a charred piece of canvas? He couldn't wrap his
mind around her actually *entering* the canvas. Maybe
she had some kind of ESP. That, added to a vivid artist's
imagination, could have conjured up those clues.

Paxton Gardner had a house on a hill overlooking
Santa Fe. No doubt the houses in town had been too
small for him, so he'd built himself a pink adobe resi-
dence big enough that Rico couldn't even guess how
many rooms the place had. Leaving the truck outside the
side entrance, he opened the gate to find Gardner on the
Saltillo-tiled patio, feet up, reading the *Wall Street Jour-
nal*. A bottle of hundred-dollar tequila and a shot glass
were within Gardner's reach.

The man looked up from his newspaper and appeared
unsettled by the intrusion. He recovered quickly, however. "Tafoya. Things so rough you're going door-to-
door to drum up business?"

"I came to tell you that you won't get away with it."

His gray eyebrows furrowed. "Get away with what?"

"Your part in Joe Cordova's murder."

Paxton flushed a deep red and his blue eyes went cold
as ice. "You don't know what you're talking about."

"You'd be better off giving yourself up to the police
than facing me, old man."

"I'll have *you* arrested!" Gardner blustered as he reached for the cell phone near the bottle of tequila. His big fingers fumbled with it and sent the phone spinning out of reach.

Rico slapped his hand over the cell. "You're not calling anyone. I'm here to make something perfectly clear to you." He felt the vestiges of the carefully created businessman slip away, leaving in its stead the man he used to be. Wearing a deadly smile, he moved in closer on the big man who looked not so big when he was sweating. "Should anything—and I mean *anything*—happen to Charlotte Reyna or anyone else who cared about Joe, *you* will not be safe from *me*. Trust me, Gardner, you don't want to be my enemy."

Gardner crushed himself back into his chair away from Rico and gaped. "Get away from me!"

An evil chuckle escaping him, Rico stood. "I'm glad you understand me."

"You're the one who doesn't understand. No one is safe against the dark forces, not even you, Tafoya."

"Is that a threat?" Rico asked. "Because I don't like threats. And if you killed Joe Cordova, you will pay. That's a promise. Your money won't get you a pass this time."

With that, Rico swept around to see Raul Estevez standing just inside the gate, his eyes bugged out. Apparently the potter had witnessed the unpleasant confrontation.

Rico shoved the potter back through the opening toward his truck stacked with his wares. "What the hell are you doing here?"

"I was gonna see if the big-shot collector wanted more of my pots, but if he had anything to do with Joe's death, no way will I trade with him."

"I don't have proof," Rico admitted, "but Gardner

knows more than he's been saying. My instincts tell me the man is guilty of something. Whatever it is, I'll get it out of him."

Raul's brow furrowed and in a low voice he said, "If you think he killed Joe, then I want a piece of him, too. Just tell me what to do and I'll help you find the proof."

Rico nodded absently. Committed to nailing Joe's murderer, he would do whatever it took....

Chapter Six

Figuring she would be in danger until the murders were solved made Charlotte realize that her life was in her own hands.

Or in Joe's...

"You're sure you're feeling better?" she asked her grandmother, who might be up and around in the kitchen area and cooking, but still didn't look herself.

"I just needed more rest. You run along and do whatever it is you must do."

Deciding not to bother Grandmother with the canvas fragment, after all, Charlotte kissed the old woman's cheek. "You can read me like a book."

Amused laughter followed Charlotte out of the room and eased the knot in her chest. Rico had been right. Just age catching up with Grandmother, that was all.

Charlotte entered her small bedroom and set the canvas fragment on her easel. Again that curious warmth when she touched it. Wanting to be comfortable, she changed into loose cargo pants and a white cotton T-shirt before sitting cross-legged on the narrow single bed. There she stared at the brush strokes on the small piece of canvas with the same intensity as she had at the ones in Joe's paintings.

Nothing.

Nearly half an hour went by during which she relaxed, cleared her mind, even envisioned some of what she had seen the last time, but nothing kick-started her into another vision. Staring at the fragment, she mentally filled in the missing part of the painting. When she touched the canvas, a feeling sizzled from her warmed fingers straight into her mind.

She had to go to the place in the painting.

Charlotte didn't like it, but she would do it. She slipped the piece of canvas back into the folder and walked into the living area to find the room empty, though a fat burrito sat on the counter awaiting her. One whiff of the delicious smell and her stomach did a little dance. She grabbed a paper towel and wrapped it around the food, then grabbed a bottle of water from the fridge. She might as well eat while she drove.

"I'm going out for a while," she called, not wanting to give details that might worry her grandmother.

Returning to the canyon that had proved dangerous wasn't the smartest thing she'd ever done, but Charlotte felt compelled to do so—not just for Joe, but for the dead janitor and for herself and for anyone else who might fall victim to the murderer. Whether she liked it or not, she'd tapped into some kind of black magic and she had to play out the hand dealt her. And she wouldn't be able to focus her energies with someone watching her back.

This time she would concentrate…not let phantom birds get to her…not step somewhere she shouldn't. If someone was using magic against her, she would fight it.

On the drive, Charlotte distracted herself by eating the burrito. A full stomach made her feel considerably better. So by the time she arrived at the canyon, she was feeling positive and strong and unwilling to be waylaid. She grabbed the envelope and a portable easel from the back and headed into the canyon, checking every foot of desert floor as she went so as not to make a mistake.

When she got to the right spot, Charlotte set her easel on a rock and pulled the canvas piece forth. Touching it made her fingers even warmer than before.

Warmer and pulsing as if the canvas had a heartbeat.

Joe's heartbeat?

Her own pulse quickened as she attached the piece to her easel and lined it up so that what was left of the painting reflected what she was seeing of the true landscape. She stared for but a moment before reality shifted slightly, her mind filling in the missing part of the painting, this time without her prompting. The rocks to one side…the arroyo slashing across the canvas…the cliff threatening to topple in on the canyon…

SUDDENLY she is walking across the desert floor.

Her heart thuds as she peers around, scrutinizing every inch of the landscape. Bits of brush…a crack in the rimrock…a snake of water trickling down the arroyo and then abruptly stopping…

She steps forward, her eyes glued to the undulating water, and ignores a skittering sound no doubt meant to distract her. The water is pointing to something, but what? Rounding a rock formation so that she has a clear look at the arroyo, she stops and lets her eyes do the traveling until they come to rest on a smooth surface wedged into the rough earth.

Moving closer, she sees the object more clearly and stoops to retrieve it. A pottery shard.

She turns it in her hands, examining it with wonder. It's ancient...and if she's not mistaken...Anasazi! Even as she identifies its ancient origins, the smell of burned canvas distracts her. She concentrates harder...finds her way deeper...perceives she is not alone!

Sensing someone behind her, she whips around to catch movement that stays just to the far edge of her vision. She's no longer in the canyon but on property she's never seen before. Then flames catch her focus. Joe's canvases in a heap on the ground...burning. Behind them, a dark figure taunts her. But try as she might, she can't get a clear view.

The skittering sound returns, accompanied by a howl...

THE ANIMAL CRY suddenly snapped Charlotte out of the trance only to have movement tease the very edge of her vision. The flesh along her spine rose and her stomach knotted.

The fear wasn't gone, because she knew she wasn't alone.

That same horrible feeling that had taken hold of her in the dangerous gallery vision threatened her now. Someone she couldn't see was out here. Someone who meant her harm.

The sun had set. Turning in a circle, she tried to pierce the nightmarish shadows around her. She shivered and rubbed her arms, as much with fright as with chill.

Charlotte grabbed the canvas with hands that trembled and shoved it back into the folder, all the while continuing to sweep her frightened gaze around the darkening landscape. Her heart was pounding so hard and loud that she nearly missed the *click-click* of nails against rock.

Spooked, she whipped around to catch a glimpse of a coyote slipping behind an old juniper.

A coyote or a shape-shifter?

With the wind at her heels, Charlotte ran for all she was worth. But the wind brought with it other noises… whispers…snicks…howls… Suddenly the air was filled with a cacophony of sound, and her head began to whirl. She threw her hands to her ears, but the sounds inside her head merely grew in volume and intensity until she couldn't tolerate listening another moment.

Her step faltered and her vision went cockeyed and the world suddenly tilted and went black…

Sometime later Charlotte's eyes fluttered open. How long had she been out? She registered the dark…the cold, hard ground beneath her…and the dark silhouette standing over her.

"Ohmigod!" she gasped, back-crabbing away from him until she realized the man was Rico. "How did you—?"

"—know where to find you?" He stepped closer, his expression grim. "I went to Sena Pueblo but I didn't see your SUV. Something told me you were pushing your luck."

He held a hand out to her. She took it to lever herself to her feet, but when she tried to let go, he wouldn't allow it.

"You aren't hurt, are you?"

She tested her limbs. "No, I'm fine." Physically. But what had happened to her mind?

"What happened?" His voice a bit gentler, Rico echoed her very thoughts.

Only she didn't exactly know. Confusion still clouded her thoughts.

"I—I had to come out here with the burned canvas. I got nothing back at the pueblo. But here…Joe was trying to tell me something." She peered around and tried to figure out what exactly. "I was interrupted." Steeling herself lest he make fun of her again, she said, "Rico, I'm certain a black witch is involved with Joe's murder."

The landscape looked innocent now, cast in a deep blue glow from a waning moon, but this place was anything but innocent. Still, she no longer felt the evil presence and was equally certain the danger had passed for the moment.

Why would the *brujo* have left?

"I'm not afraid of any child's nightmare, Charlotte."

She shivered. "I swear to you the evil is real. It's gone now, but I faced it and it terrified me."

The next thing she knew she was flat against Rico's chest and his arms were around her.

"I won't let evil touch you."

Drawn to his warmth, to the protective gesture, she didn't try to pull away, not even when he tightened his hold on her. She was glad not to be alone, for she knew what she had faced here just a short time ago. His heart beat against her chest…and his erection pressed against her thighs.

So quickly that it made her head spin, Rico let go of her and said, "C'mon, let's get out of here."

Charlotte merely nodded, but when he stepped off, trying to pull her with him, she stood firm. "Wait."

"What's wrong?"

"The folder…I—I don't see it."

Her gaze skittered along the moonlit ground and back the way she had come before passing out. Maybe it just blended with the earth. Rico clicked on a flashlight. A waste of time.

"It's gone…the evidence is gone," she said, feeling responsible. "That's why he left."

"Who?"

"The *brujo*. He got what he wanted from me…and then you arrived. I guess he didn't want to deal with both of us."

"That's one explanation," Rico agreed, taking her hand and leading her back in the direction of their parked vehicles.

But when Rico's truck came into view, Charlotte looked around at the familiar rock formations but didn't see her SUV.

"I thought I parked right here."

"You did. That's how I found you. Looks like you ran into a thief."

Something far worse, Charlotte decided. Rico was sweeping his flashlight around, as if looking for footprints. Suddenly his curse filled the night.

"What the hell! The bastard slashed my tires!"

Her car was gone and his had been disabled so they couldn't go after the villain. Obviously the witch was buying himself time by keeping them here. Wondering what evil he was up to now, Charlotte shivered.

Rico tried to call to get help, but his cell didn't pick up a signal. Neither did hers.

"We're going to have to walk back," Charlotte said.

"Not in the dark."

"Then what?"

"We wait for first light. The desert can be dangerous at night."

Charlotte's finely tuned senses told her the biggest danger was out of the picture for the moment—she would sense the black witch if he were still around—

but she didn't want to argue with Rico. She was stressed out enough.

As if he sensed her emotions, he took her in his arms and rubbed a hand down the length of her spine. The gesture was meant to be soothing, she knew, but instead he was quickly arousing her.

"It won't be so bad," he murmured into her hair. "I have a sleeping bag in the pickup, and there's plenty of room in the back to stretch out. If you get cold, I'll be here to keep you warm."

Charlotte sighed. "Rico…thanks for coming after me. Twice. If you hadn't…"

She would be out here alone.

Rico gently cupped the back of her head and looked deep into her eyes. His features went taut as his head swooped lower and his lips tangled with hers in a passionate kiss. The heat that sizzled along her nerves was so intense that Charlotte admitted to herself what she had known underneath all along. Despite their differences, she wanted Rico. And from the way his body was continuing to respond to her, he desired her equally.

Hoping to drive all bad thoughts from her mind for a while, she used her body to tell Rico what she wanted. He jammed her back against the side of the truck, then pulled his mouth from hers with a gasp.

"Are you sure?" was all he asked.

"I'm yours if you want me."

Rico didn't hesitate. Kissing her again, he danced her lip-locked to the back of the pickup. Without losing a beat, he somehow opened the gate. Then he had to free her long enough to boost her inside. He followed, found the sleeping bag and set out the makeshift bed.

Charlotte pulled off her boots and wiggled out of her

cargo pants, leaving only her T-shirt and panties. Rico did the same, only he wasn't wearing any underwear.

A moment later they were stretched out on the sleeping bag, kissing, touching each other. Charlotte unbraided his hair so it flowed around her face. Rico found her breasts unbound under the T-shirt and thumbed her nipples into turgid peaks.

"No bra? A fashion statement?" he asked softly, then without waiting for a response, slipped the T-shirt up so he could taste her.

When he took her nipple deep into his mouth, Charlotte moaned with the pleasure. Her hips began moving to the rhythm of his tongue. His hand slipped down her stomach, making her quake, and then inside the front of her panties. She gasped as he kept going. She was ready for him, wet and slick, and he slid a finger deep inside her. Then he was licking his way down her stomach, with his free hand tugging at her panties until they twisted around her knees. His tongue sliding along her clit made her raise her hips and cry out.

She grabbed handfuls of his long hair and tried to pull his head up to hers so he could slide inside her, but he wasn't having any. She sensed rather than saw his grin as he continued pleasuring her.

Barely a moment later she came in giant sweeping waves.

When she settled, breathing hard, he finished removing her panties and snaked over her, the undulating movement arousing her all over again. She spread her thighs for him and he slid into her as though he belonged there.

In those brief seconds before she became caught up in the frantic rhythm of their lovemaking, Charlotte looked up at the night sky full of stars and convinced herself that anything was possible. She and Rico could resolve their differences, and with one heart and mind and soul fight the evil that needed to be stopped.

Chapter Seven

At first light, Rico was already indulging himself in Charlotte. Not that he was making love to her again; he was watching her sleep and thinking how lovely and talented and brave she was. And foolish, of course, though she wouldn't appreciate the last.

What made a woman like her—one who could fit in anywhere, even with the east coast upper crust—come back to live such a simple life? For him, the life hadn't been as simple as had been his choice to leave it.

Charlotte's eyes blinked open and in them he read surprise…puzzlement…warmth. His pulse threaded unevenly in response.

"Morning. I hope you're well rested. We have quite a walk ahead of us."

"Maybe you should have let me sleep last night."

"Is that what you wanted?"

"You gave me exactly what I wanted." Her voice was husky, her smile dazzling.

Rico brushed her mouth with his and ignored the renewed urgings to have her a fourth time. Sex could wait. Safety couldn't. He wanted to get her back to civilization, such as the pueblo provided. Or perhaps now he could convince her to stay with him. Better yet, to move in permanently.

The thought of waking up every morning to that smile warmed him.

As they dressed, Charlotte said, "I've been thinking."

"About?"

"About what Joe was trying to tell me in my vision. I was led to a shard of ancient pottery that I would swear was Anasazi."

"Not uncommon out here," Rico said, still not knowing what to make of her so-called visions.

She gave him an annoyed look. "And directly after that, I jumped to another place, one I hadn't seen before."

"Another canyon?"

"No. Someone's property. I saw a small house…and Joe's paintings in a heap on the ground…burning."

Of course she had. She'd just learned about them being burned and had brought the charred piece of canvas out here. That had filled her imagination.

Still he tried to be tactful. "So what do you think it all means?"

"That there's a connection between the paintings and the pottery I held in my hands."

"You mean, like a clue to the identity of the murderer? Not very specific considering how many potters work on Sena Pueblo alone."

But Charlotte was shaking her head. "No, that's not what I mean. I told you the pottery was old."

"Yeah, but you can interpret that however you want."

"That's what you think I'm doing? Interpreting things the way *I* want?"

Uh-oh. "I think we should discuss this over breakfast." She would surely be more reasonable on a full stomach.

"Now *there's* an assumption—that I would want to have breakfast with you."

"Wait a minute, Charlotte. Just because I'm not going along with everything you say a hundred percent, you're angry?"

"You're not going along with anything I'm telling you."

His own irritation kicked in. "You have to admit this vision thing, the way you describe it, is pretty farfetched and open to interpretation. Not just yours."

Charlotte stared at him as if she didn't recognize him. Rico's chest squeezed, but he wasn't going to tell her he believed in Pueblo mumbo-jumbo simply to humor her. He'd divorced himself from all that when he'd made a new world for himself. She couldn't expect him to do an about-face just on her say-so.

"I was right about you when I said you don't believe in anything or anyone. You are a big disappointment to me, Rico Tafoya."

With that, she started the long trek back to town.

CHARLOTTE COULDN'T WAIT to get home and away from Rico. After what they'd shared the night before, she'd expected him to at least give her the benefit of the doubt. She swallowed hard. He didn't believe her. He didn't believe in *brujos* or spiritual journeys or magic. He'd simply been playing neutral so as not to upset her.

How had she thought they could be of one heart and mind and soul?

Luckily, Rico tried his cell phone again and magically it began working. An old friend of Rico's drove out to meet them a third of the way back, so they were spared the long walk. Whether she liked it or not, however, she was crushed between the two men. Too close to Rico for her comfort, considering the way she was feeling.

Suddenly she spotted a dusty red vehicle abandoned on the side of the road.

"My SUV! Stop!"

The truck pulled over. Rico got out and offered her a hand. Clenching her jaw, she took it, but she let go the moment her feet were on solid ground.

Checking out her SUV, she was relieved that there didn't seem to be a scratch on it. She opened the driver's door and the keys were in the ignition.

"Hey, wait a minute," Rico said. "You better leave it. There might be prints."

"Yeah, I just had some work done, so there might be a lot of prints of different people who could be implicated. Or maybe none at all…at least none that belong to the witch. Besides, how seriously do you think Gonzales will take me, Rico, when *you* think I'm a joke?"

"You're exaggerating."

"As usual, right?" she asked coolly.

He didn't answer but stood glaring at her as she climbed behind the wheel.

"What do you plan on doing?" he asked.

"I don't know." She started the engine. "Yes, I do. I'm going to talk this thing through with Grandmother. *She* believes in me. You'd better get your truck hauled in and the tires repaired."

With a chill between them, Charlotte drove for home, regretting she couldn't keep her grandmother out of this. She needed the wise old woman's guidance, since it was clear that only through a journey of more power than she possessed would the face of evil be revealed.

Entering the house, she was surprised to find the living area empty. Grandmother was usually up at dawn, cooking or cleaning.

Charlotte went to her bedroom and knocked on the door. She thought she heard a faint "Come in."

Opening the door, she frowned when she saw her grandmother still in bed. "What's wrong?"

"Weak...dizzy."

Charlotte rushed to her side. "Did you call the doctor? Let me help you up. I'll take you to the clinic."

"No, white man's medicine can do nothing for me." Grandmother clasped Charlotte's wrist. "He was here... in the shadows."

"Who?"

"The witch. *Brujo*."

Charlotte's heart began to pound. "You saw him?"

"Felt him...at first not sure...but last night he returned...knows I tried to help poor Roberto...doesn't want me to help *you*, Granddaughter."

Charlotte tried to keep it together. "Do you know the witch's identity?"

Grandmother shook her head. "Many years ago, before you were born, Joe Cordova and some of the other young men in the pueblo flirted around with the dark arts. Something scared Joe off. That doesn't mean he forgot."

"But Joe's dead."

"His magic calls you from his paintings. The black witch knows this."

"Joe put magic in his paintings? But how?"

"He must have painted while both in a vision and yet aware...a powerful and dangerous journey..."

Grandmother was out of breath and looking weaker by the minute.

"Tell me what to do to help you."

"Do as Joe did...only way to fight the *brujo*..."

Feeling panicked at the thought of trying to manipulate the dream state, Charlotte tried not to show it. She kissed the old woman's leathery cheek. "I'll have Lurene come to stay with you."

As she started to rise, her grandmother grabbed her by the wrist. Her voice was a hoarse whisper when she said, "Not alone. Be safe, Granddaughter. I will chant for you."

Swallowing hard, Charlotte nodded. Then she turned around and saw Rico at the door.

RICO HAD CALLED a service to go out and get his truck for him, after which he'd come straight to Charlotte's place to square things with her. Just what he wanted to hear—Dolores Reyna giving her granddaughter instructions on how to put herself in more danger.

He refrained from saying anything until Charlotte made that call and told him, "Her neighbor Lurene will see to Grandmother until I return."

"And who will see to you?"

"I *had* hoped it might be you."

"You want me to put my stamp of approval on your putting yourself in danger again?"

"I have no choice."

"We all have choices."

"And you made yours, Rico, years ago. And you're so rigid you can't even try to open your mind. There's just something I don't understand."

"There's a lot I don't understand—"

"How could you hate your own people enough to refuse to believe what's right under your nose?"

"That's the problem, it isn't under my nose!" he shouted.

This wasn't going as he'd planned. He'd hoped to find the right words to pacify Charlotte, to recapture some of the warmth and passion that had been better than anything he could put a name to. Instead they were increasingly at odds.

"But I'm telling you it *is* under your nose," she said. "You refuse to open your mind because your heart is so heavy with prejudice against the old ways that you would see someone else die rather than believe me."

A knock at the door interrupted the argument. Charlotte let her neighbor Lurene in and led her to the old woman's bedroom.

Rico fidgeted until she came out. He wanted to say something to heal this breach between them, but he didn't trust his own words. Charlotte began gathering her paints and a canvas—a landscape she'd been working on.

"What are you doing?"

"I'm going to save Grandmother…and anyone else from the witch."

Frustrated and angry, Rico watched her leave. He wanted to go after her, but he didn't have the right words. He figured he would continue to make things worse.

"Rico…"

Rico whipped around to see Charlotte's grandmother standing in the doorway, supported by the neighbor.

"Mrs. Reyna, should you be out of bed?"

"You must go after her, Rico. If you don't, you could lose her for good."

"I think I've already done that." And the idea was killing him.

"Charlotte intends to face the *brujo,* but she's not strong enough yet. Alone, she is vulnerable."

Damn! Rico couldn't let Charlotte get hurt—or worse—no matter what he believed. "All right, I'll go after her. What about you? Should I call a doctor?"

"Lurene will stay with me until it is done."

Done? What did that mean? Rico decided he'd better not wait for an explanation. Nodding to the old woman, he ran out of the house only to remember he had no vehicle.

Thinking he could get Charlotte faster if he cut across land too rough even for an SUV, Rico borrowed a horse from a guy who lived at the edge of town. Who would ever believe he would be on a horse again, cutting across pueblo land…only one person could make him do this…could make him doubt his own disbelief in Pueblo magic.

He loved Charlotte too much to let her face danger alone.

A black witch.

His stomach twisted. He hadn't forgotten the stories of witches and shape-shifters of his youth. He hadn't forgotten what a *brujo* could do to an enemy.

The stuff of Pueblo tales spoken to children…and yet, part of him couldn't shut off his growing fear for Charlotte…the woman he loved…

Chapter Eight

Charlotte slid out of the driver's seat and looked up. There had been no warning of an impending storm, but the wind had whipped up and the skies were tinted a yellowish green. A chill shot through her, but she didn't want to analyze it too closely. If it rained, it rained. This couldn't wait. Grandmother couldn't wait.

No sooner had she opened the back to get her supplies than she heard what sounded like hoofbeats. She looked around to see a pinto carrying a rider across the open plain. A figure in black that could only be Rico Tafoya.

Clenching her jaw, she pulled out her paints and easel and canvas and set off before he could stop her. He caught up to her at the mouth of the canyon. Pulling the horse around in front of her, he blocked the opening.

"Get out of my way, Rico." Her pulse was racing, whether at the challenge or simply at seeing him, she wasn't certain. "You're not going to change my mind."

"Your grandmother sent me."

Charlotte's breath caught in her throat and she choked out, "Is she all right?"

"She wasn't any worse when I left, but she's afraid for you. She said alone you would be vulnerable."

"I have to do this, Rico. If you can't understand that, I'm sorry. Besides, you don't believe in my visions anyway, so I should be perfectly safe, right?"

"Only if I'm watching over you so no one can get to you in this reality."

"Do what you must. Just get out of my way."

When he didn't immediately move, she went forward and swatted the pinto's hindquarters. The horse danced around and gave her an opening.

Charlotte was halfway down to the canyon before he caught up to her again, still on horseback. She gave him a suspicious glare, but he didn't seem to be paying her any mind. He was gazing around, glancing up at the rimrock. How obvious that he *was* trying to protect her— she told herself to appreciate the fact.

Finding her spot and setting up her easel, Charlotte eyed the darkening skies and hoped she had enough time to do what she must. She set the canvas on the easel and her box of paints on a nearby rock. The landscape she'd been working on at home almost could have been done here. A few changes in the scene and she would be in business.

Rico was leading the pinto around the canyon, checking behind every upturned boulder, every crevice.

She opened the box of paints and chose several tubes of color. But before she could prepare her palette, a sharp whistle diverted her attention.

Just ahead, Rico shot off his mount and got down on his haunches to inspect something behind one of those boulders. Charlotte thought to ignore him, but curiosity got the better of her. She set down her paints and carefully made her way to him.

"What is it?" she asked, but upon moving closer,

saw a boot poking out from behind the boulder. Her stomach clenched. "Another body?"

Rico stood. "Paxton Gardner. Dead. Looks like a heart attack."

"Ohmigod. Poor Jessie." She knew the other woman loved her father no matter how much grief he gave her.

"We need to alert the authorities."

"Not yet."

"Why would we wait?"

"I have work to do," she said, heading back for her easel.

"The murderer is dead. The threat is over. Gardner was the killer."

"You don't know that."

"We already suspected him. Why else would he be out here?"

"Shouldn't the question be, who killed him?" Charlotte asked, already intent on squeezing smears of desert brown and red and sand on her palette.

She painted quick additions to the canvas she'd already been working on—adding the cave above, the arroyo below, the boulders where Paxton Gardner's body lay to the side. All the while, she concentrated, forgot that Rico stood watching, freed her mind, guided herself to that state halfway between being awake and truly in a trance.

Then Charlotte painted herself into the canvas…

SHE LOOKS around the canyon for signs of life. Signs of evil. She doesn't see it, but she feels it around her.

Brujo! Come out and face me like a man!

At her silent challenge, the air whirls around her, as though cloaking her. A rumble of thunder precedes a

*lightning strike. She turns and turns and turns, search-
ing for the black witch. She knows he's here.*

Why won't he come out to meet her?

RICO HAD NEVER SEEN anything like this. Charlotte, eyes
open, brush poised in the air as if to make another
stroke…her mind gone to some other plane. This was
worse than the gallery. He could feel her slipping away.

His chest squeezed tight and his stomach clenched.
Delores Reyna knew the old ways and she worried that,
alone, Charlotte was vulnerable. He was here to watch
over her, but was that enough? If indeed there was a
black witch, was she strong enough to fight him alone?
What if she went so far in this journey of hers that she
couldn't come back?

Even as he realized that on some level he was ac-
knowledging what she believed, she dropped the brush
and her eyes rolled back in her head.

"Charlotte! Jesus!"

Terrified of her being hurt because he was too damn
stubborn to listen to her, Rico stared at the painting,
grasped her shoulder and tried to force his mind to a
place it didn't want to go…

*SHE SENSES she is not alone. Her gaze is drawn to the cliff
as a dark figure steps out of the cave, arms raised and
circling so that wind and lightning dance around him.*

*Her stomach clutches. What did she think she could
do alone against one with such power?*

*Another presence…this one closer. Her shoulder
burns and she glances left to see Rico at her side.*

"How did you get here?" she asks.

"I chose to believe in you."

One mind...

He takes her hand and her pulse settles into rhythm with his.

One heart...

His chest is bared but for the elaborate silver-and-turquoise necklace...the turquoise meant to ward off evil. His hips are encased in buckskin breeches. A warrior. Wind whips his long hair around his face as he stares deep into her eyes.

One soul...

Together they climb to face the black witch.

The villain raises a staff and guides a bolt of lightning in their direction. They raise their hands and the bolt shoots off to the side. Another stroke of the staff and the heavens open. Rain washes down the arroyo in an angry torrent.

CHARLOTTE BLINKED and saw the water coming for her and Rico. Her brush...where was it? Dazedly, she looked around until she found it on the ground. Rico let go of her shoulder only long enough for her to retrieve it. Quickly she dipped the bristles in color, then painted the canvas to change the arroyo's direction and divert the water.

THE WITCH comes closer.

His face is painted in ghostly black and white makeup, his hair tied in two horns flagged with corn husks. Court jester and mediator with the spirit world?

Wrong, she thinks. Rather a mask he's been using to fool everyone.

Rico grabs the witch and finds a rattler in his hand, ready to strike.

CHARLOTTE FELT her heart hit her ribs. Rico could die if the rattler struck him in the magical vision. She couldn't let that happen. Pulse jagging, she dipped her brush across her palette and quickly painted the rattler into a harmless lizard.

THE WITCH throws the lizard from him and raises his staff yet again.

Before he can harness the earth's forces, she sees through the makeup and uses the most powerful of commands—by calling his real name, she reveals his true identity.

SUDDENLY, Charlotte realized the dream was broken. She was back in the canyon, Rico still at her side.

In front of them stood the black witch in the flesh.

Chapter Nine

Rico came out of the trance with a start. He would be disbelieving if he hadn't experienced the weird scenario himself.

"You have more power than I even suspected," the black witch was saying to Charlotte.

"Back at you, Raul," Rico growled. Who would ever have expected the struggling potter to be a multiple murderer? "So you killed Joe and Roberto and Paxton—"

"Don't forget Brian Thompson," Estevez said. "He was the first. And so easy."

Thompson, too. So the bones did belong to Ashley's father.

"What did you have against these men?" Charlotte asked.

"Me and Brian and Joe found a cache of Anasazi pottery and sold off pieces to private collectors."

"Like Gardner," Rico mused, his gaze traveling over Raul to see what weapons he might be carrying. If he had any, they were well hidden. Intending to overpower the man, he waited for the right opening and let the bastard keep talking.

"Paxton Gardner's one of my best customers, the

first back when we started. Too bad Brian got a conscience and started babbling about sharing such treasures with the world. I have to admit I was in a rage when I used my power to kill him. But he had to be dealt with."

"Is that when Joe stopped dabbling in the black arts?" Charlotte asked. "Grandmother said he stopped when something scared him."

"He must've seen, whether in person or in a vision, because he refused to work with me again. Brian's disappearance was a bad omen, he said, and I let him go. We'd been friends since we were dirt-poor kids. I didn't think he'd betray me. Not until recently when he began adding those clues to our crimes into his paintings. I felt his guilt ooze off those canvases. He was feeling sorry for all the poor members of the Pueblo who weren't benefitting from that valuable pottery found on Pueblo land. I tried to scare him into stopping, but he wouldn't, the idiot."

"Give it up, Raul," Rico said. "You're finished."

"You are a fool. You have no idea of what I am. Do you think I'd be here talking to you like this if I was going to let you live?"

Rico responded with a well-placed punch and sent the miserable excuse for a human being flying.

Raul caught himself as he fell and lunged at Rico, who took a couple of punches to the middle that had him out of breath. The little bastard was strong for his size.

Seemingly out of nowhere, Raul produced a knife.

"Rico, look out!" Charlotte cried.

Raul must have had some mind-hold on a bunch of people, Rico thought, but not on him. The potter didn't look scary, but whatever had just happened between the three of them in their minds had been terrifying.

Rico said, "When messing with Joe's mind didn't work, you killed him and destroyed all the canvases you could find."

"I knew it was only a matter of time before someone else saw those clues in his paintings. You, it seems," Raul again said to Charlotte.

Slipping his own knife from the holster inside his boot, Rico said, "Lucky for me, I always look out for myself."

They circled each other, Raul lunging forward ineffectively a couple of times, Rico watching him carefully. The potter had more anger than skill in his use of the weapon. Rico waited for an opening, then moved in, nicking Raul's knife hand with his blade. Raul cursed and dropped his knife. Rico kicked it away and considered finishing the bastard, but he'd never before taken a life. So he tossed his knife to the side and began to pummel Raul with his fists until the man backed away under the onslaught.

"Your fists are nothing compared to my power!" Raul shouted, then started mumbling something in the Keres language too fast for Rico to follow.

CHARLOTTE TOLD herself not to panic. She understood Raul's power even if Rico didn't. If Rico so much as let up for an instant, the witch could kill him using black magic. She didn't understand Keres, but she recognized his intent.

She had to help Rico and knew only one way.

Picking up her palette and brush, she painted both male figures into the canvas, then concentrated, seeking that state of dream and awareness...

SUDDENLY she is on the sidelines, watching.

Warrior and witch are equally matched until the witch conjures a bolt of lightning in his hand.

She knows he will use this to kill Rico, to make it look like a heart attack.

QUICKLY, Charlotte cut a swath of paint through the bolt, disabling it.

The witch knows she is there. He holds out his arms and shouts at them both in Keres. The winds begin to whip around him. The sky above darkens to black…the clouds stretch…the earth rumbles beneath her feet.

He is gathering his power!

How to stop him?

Before the witch had time to act, she painted restraints around his body so quickly she felt as if magic were guiding her hand.

"You will not move…"

A gag around his mouth.

"…you will not utter a curse…"

A binding around his head.

"…and you will not will evil!"

She looked up again just as Rico delivered a blow that knocked Raul out cold.

"It is done," she murmured.

"Yeah, he's done for, all right."

It was over, Charlotte realized. She was free of the dream state and fully in the present. She could breathe easily again.

Rico whistled for the pinto and fetched the rope tied to the horse's saddle. He used it on Raul as she had done to the witch in the painting.

Then Rico rose and took a trembling Charlotte in his arms.

"You're safe now," he said.

"We're all safe."

They delivered a still unconscious Raul Estevez to the tribal police and reported finding Paxton Gardner dead, and that Raul had admitted to killing the man.

Waiting for the ambulance to arrive, Charlotte told Fred Gonzales, "He's *brujo*. I stopped him in a vision, but I don't know how long that will last."

Rather than tell her she was crazy, as Charlotte expected, Gonzales crossed himself and mumbled something as he hurried off. One of the junior officers took their statements.

Afterward, as they left to check on Charlotte's grandmother, Rico asked, "You think you're the one who stopped him?"

"I bound him so he wouldn't be able to use his magic against you."

"My knuckles say differently."

Of course. He'd had a moment of weakness when he'd let her take him into the dreamworld, but now he was back to being disbelieving.

When they walked into the *casita*, Grandmother was up and in the kitchen alone.

"You're all right!" Charlotte rushed over to envelope the small woman in her arms.

"A miracle. It seemed I was to leave this earth and then, just a while ago, the fever magically left me. I am myself."

"A while ago…when I figured out a way to stop the witch from casting his evil net," Charlotte said. "I'm so glad. I only hope the black witch is gone forever."

Charlotte turned to see what Rico had to say about it, but he wasn't there.

He'd gone without telling her he was leaving.

"He'll be back," Grandmother said.

Charlotte wasn't so sure. Rico had divorced himself from everything Pueblo long ago. Their experience had no doubt freaked him out. And hearing her claim responsibility for stopping the witch might just have pushed him over the edge away from her.

A lump suddenly lodged in her throat at the loss and her chest squeezed tight. "Grandmother, do you mind if I paint for a while?"

"No need to fuss about me. I have my life because of you. Now go."

Before the image in her head slipped away from her, Charlotte wanted to paint. Another kiss on Grandmother's cheek and she ran outside to the SUV to get her tools.

She would seek solace in the only thing left to her that could make her feel whole.

THE NEXT MORNING, Charlotte rose with the sun and after eating a hurried breakfast went out to the small courtyard in back where she continued working on her newest, most inspired piece. She'd chosen a canyon she'd already painted as the background—not Joe's canyon, for she wanted no reminder of the evil that had bred there over the decades—but one of the areas familiar to her own landscapes.

She thought of Joe as she worked, though, both with sadness and a great gladness that she had known him, even if for a short while. He had opened her artist's mind and she had let in this enchanted land. They both would hold a place in her soul forever.

The day before she'd painted in the full-length ghost figure in fleshtone, then had started to add in details. Buckskin breeches, silver-and-turquoise squash blossom necklace, long, loose hair around his question mark of a face.

Normally an artist doing a portrait works from photographs or sketches of the subject, but it would have been impossible to get either in this instance. So by necessity, Charlotte was working from memory. She concentrated…sought the half-awake dream state she'd entered when fighting the witch so she could once more conjure her reluctant warrior.

Suddenly she could see Rico's rugged tanned face in her mind. She painted the high cheekbones…the straight blade of a nose…the full lips that rarely curved in a smile. The portrait was coming together with breathtaking quickness. She added the small details, the shadows and curves, and left the eyes for last.

After taking a break, she went back to the canvas and stared at it for a while. Thought maybe this was all she had to remember him by. The real Rico Tafoya, not the one who disguised himself in black, hair pulled from his strong mestizo face. This showed who he really was inside.

Back to work.

She sketched in the eyes, colored the centers with dabs of pale green the exact shade of Rico's irises. Unable to get the shape of the lids just right, she cursed under her breath.

"Having trouble with your painting?"

Charlotte looked up to find those very green eyes in front of her. Rico in the flesh.

Her pulse picked up but she tried to sound natural when she said, "Having trouble with my subject."

Thinking she could take advantage of his being here, she began making tiny alterations on the eyes in the painting. Better than thinking about what wasn't meant to be.

"I was just at the hospital. I thought you'd like to know Raul is in some kind of a coma."

That stopped Charlotte cold for a moment. "What are his chances?"

"They're not saying yet."

Which made her wonder what she should do about the canvas. She'd wanted to stop the witch, but she hadn't counted on this. Should she change it to release a man who'd murdered at least four men and maybe others? She couldn't ask Rico's opinion. He would scoff at her, of course, because he didn't believe in anything beyond his five senses.

Putting the dilemma to the back of her mind for the moment, knowing she would have to resolve it later, she realized Rico's gaze was on her. He seemed so intent.

"You're not blaming yourself, are you?"

"Blaming…oh, you mean Raul. No, I was thinking about something else altogether."

"Something else?"

"Us." He moved closer and stood over her.

"I'm not sure there is an us, Rico."

He didn't immediately respond and she realized he was staring at the canvas. She tried to read him, to know what he was feeling as he looked at himself—if he even recognized himself.

"Is that what you want me to look like?"

"A warrior? I suppose so. It's how I saw you yesterday."

"In the vision?"

She nodded and waited for him to make a hurtful comment.

Instead he said, "I'm sorry I doubted you, Charlotte. I can't explain what happened yesterday…but I know what I experienced. It scared the living daylights out of me. That's why I left—to think without you distracting me. I thought about it all night. I thought about you. About how brave you were. About how you saved my life."

"Rico, we did it together. You put yourself in danger for me, too, and even if for a short time, you went beyond your own prejudices and became one with me."

Which made her think there was great hope for him yet.

"I would like to become one with you at any time..." he murmured, his expression hopeful. "And at all times if you'll have me."

Only days ago she would never have believed she would hear those words from Rico. She would never have believed how deeply they touched her. But he had changed. Not completely perhaps, but enough that his words made her heart sing with hope for the future.

"I'll have you, Rico...heart, mind and soul."

"Don't forget the body," he said, taking her in his arms.

"That, too," she murmured just as his lips met hers.

Epilogue

"So who's the hunk?" The blond woman wearing an incredible turquoise necklace and bracelets set in gold rather than silver glanced from the painting of Rico to the man himself.

"I saw him in my mind," Charlotte said, "and I fell in love with him. That's why he's not for sale."

The woman sighed, sipped at her flute of champagne and went on to the next painting. To Charlotte's delight and awe, several already had big Sold signs on them.

"Who said I'm not for sale?" Rico murmured in her hair. "I'll be yours tonight for the right price."

Charlotte raised her eyebrows. "And what might that be?"

"Move in with me."

"Hmm. Tempting. Let me think about it."

"You've had three months to think."

"Have you been bored?"

Before Rico could respond, Jay signaled him. "I'll be right back."

Three months had passed since their encounter with the black witch. Charlotte had repainted the canvas, had removed the bindings on the figure representing Raul, but the man was still in a coma. Grandmother had visited him in the hospital and had assured Charlotte that his own evil kept Raul trapped inside his head. If he were ever to come out of it, he would be tried for multiple murders.

In the meantime, Charlotte had been inspired when painting. Her dreamworld had transferred itself to her canvases. Tonight the Milagro Gallery was filled with the elite of Santa Fe, all here to celebrate *her.* The art critic for the Santa Fe *Sun* had said her work was magic. He didn't know the half of it. Charlotte couldn't get over the thrill but was glad friends had come to ground her.

"I'm so happy for you," Ashley said. She was glued to her new husband's side—she and Luke had married on that trip to see her parents, who had given their full approval of the match. "And I'm relieved that Joe lives on, too."

"Thank God, Rico was able to find someone to restore those mutilated canvases," Luke said.

Charlotte was proud that Rico had given Joe a wall of his own. "Joe deserves to be remembered."

"He was so kind," Ashley said. "He even remembered me in his will. He left me some land he bought from my biological father."

The DNA results had proved that the man who'd been killed in the desert—Brian Thompson—was, indeed, her father.

"We're going to donate the land to the pueblo—for low-cost housing that Luke is going to build. Which will also provide jobs and job training for local men."

Luke's attention was diverted. "Hey, Tom…Jessie…" He waved over the newly arrived couple.

Charlotte was relieved to see that Jessie was looking happy for once. She'd had a difficult time accepting her father's murder, but it seemed she was recovering. "Good to see you both."

"I don't know much about art except what I like," Tom said. "I *love* this."

Jessie said, "You so deserve all the good things in your future."

"You, as well," Charlotte said.

"I have the best." Jessie held up her left hand and wiggled the ring finger, where an oval diamond caught the light.

"You're engaged! Congratulations!" Charlotte waved over a waiter with the champagne.

Rico arrived in time to toast the happy couple, then dragged Charlotte off behind the embroidered deerskin.

"Now about that price we were negotiating…"

"Move in with you? Nothing else will do?"

"Let's call it a start," Rico said.

"Let's."

Though she wasn't really psychic, Charlotte knew their future was together.

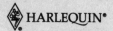
HARLEQUIN®

INTRIGUE

Return to

McCALLS' MONTANA

**this spring
with**

B.J. DANIELS

Their land stretched for miles across
the Big Sky state…all of it hard-earned—
none of it negotiable. Could family ties
withstand the weight of lasting legacy?

AMBUSHED!
May

HIGH-CALIBER COWBOY
June

SHOTGUN SURRENDER
July

Available wherever Harlequin Books are sold.

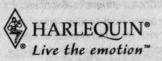

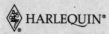

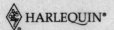